RECKLESS RAPTURE

STOLEN LEGACY, BOOK FOUR

CANDICE BUNDY

PIPER FOX

CONTENTS

DO I STAY OR SHOULD I GO?

SERA

With an elegant whoosh, Taneisha's portal deposited the posse and I at the front steps of Franc's posh nightclub, Velvet. The large, rectangular black building rose from the black pavement with hardly a window in evidence. In the dark of night, I couldn't get a sense of how big the building was from the outside. The only noteworthy element was the flickering pink neon sign reflected off everything metal and shiny, including a few shallow puddles through the parking lot. Still holding Liam's hand, I sauntered across the pavement under a cloudy, moonlit sky up to the wide-open black doors.

With each step away from the portal, a flush of magic flared through my veins. The icy cold sensation was followed by a rush of heat a moment later. It was almost as if I had numbed fingers from standing outside in the cold too long, only to feel my flesh burning as the blood returned in a heated rush to my extremities. My skin exuded an unnatural, pale glow as the rebounding return of my magic refused to be confined to my mortal form.

Despite my relief at feeling the power running through me, fear gripped my heart. Unlike the prestige it usually conveyed for mages, my magic had never been a blessing, but more of a chaotic curse.

Fearing for what my magic might do to the wolf-shifter, I tried to pull my hand from Liam's grasp. He held firm, his eyes lighting up as he grinned from ear to ear. "Your magic is back!"

"Here I thought for a moment that you were just aglow from the neon, but I'm glad to see Taneisha kept her word about returning your magic," Franc said.

I held up my free hand, a ball of electric mage fire springing to life at my command. I let out a slow sigh. "Let's hope you're in the mood to play nice today," I muttered to the ball of energy before I extinguished it with a flick of my fingers. "That's one more edge we can count in our court for this quest." The glow around my skin began to fade, which I assumed meant my body was adapting to the return of my magic.

At least, so I'd heard. I'd never been here before, not beyond when Emrys had dragged me here a couple of days ago at the start of this series of quests with the posse. I couldn't deny a fascination with what I might find inside. This wasn't just a hip nightclub; it was a view into Franc that I hadn't seen before.

Franc paused at Velvet's front doors, and I had the impression he was steeling himself for whatever we'd find inside. This was his club, a place dedicated to the modern worship of Dionysus. I imagined this place fed the demigod's needs on magical, social, and financial levels.

Through the doorway and past the entry, I could make out the bump and grind of bodies grooving to the music under the steady beat. It sounded exactly like what I'd expect, yet Franc's sour expression gave me pause.

"You look worried." I pulled away from Liam and leaned up against his arm. The night air hovered somewhere between chill and cool, and in the barely there champagne sparkly dress which Taneisha had dressed me in, I craved the heat of his touch.

"I'm not worried," Franc replied, not turning to look at me. "I'm pissed. I don't know whether I'm more upset over retrieving the divine mask of Dionysos or concerned over what damage the partying masses may have done to Velvet in my absence. No one should have been able to even get in without my permission!"

"Taneisha must have breached the magical wards you have which control the guest list. That's the only way anyone would have been able to enter. Whatever damage she's done, or the partiers have done, we'll sort it out," Marcos said, placing a reassuring hand on Franc's shoulder. He'd worked at Franc's bouncer ever since the club had opened, so no doubt he already had a mental game plan to sort out the club. "This is Velvet. It's yours, even if you've been away, and even if a fae has brought in a horde of trolls. We've had things go sideways before, and it's never been something you couldn't handle or bring back from the ashes."

Although I figured Marcos was kidding about the trolls, it got me wondering. What dangers might lie inside? What creatures? Taneisha had no desire to make this easy on us, so there had to be something up her sleeve. Most likely multiple somethings.

"I hope that's the case." Franc frowned, but then turned his focus on me, pinning me with the full intensity of his blue-eyed gaze. "I want you to go home."

My breath caught in my throat. His gaze traveled over my face before dipping down to linger on the lines of my body. It felt like he was memorizing what I looked like just in case he might not see me again. "What? No. I just got my magic back and I assure you I'm ready to rumble."

Franc's smile was bitter. "We're back in our reality, Sera. From here, you can call a ride and go home. Whatever Taneisha has planned for us in there, at least then I'd know you're safe."

Liam's hand caught mine again, and I turned to him in disbelief. "As much as I'd hate to be parted from you, Franc's idea is sound. This is an opportunity for you to get away from the fae and stay safe."

I ground my teeth together, pulling away from Liam again. Whatever I'd expected heading into this next quest, it wasn't this. Did they really think I'd tap out and leave them at Taneisha's mercy? Heck, she seemed to like me. I was the safest one here from the fae.

I planted my hands on my hips, pivoting back to look at Caden and Emrys. "You guys in agreement?"

Emrys replied with a brooding nod. "I'd feel better if you weren't at risk. Let me call you a ride?" He pointed to a phone box at the corner of the building with the letters FREE RIDES stenciled in white over the box.

I mean, if I'd been looking for a sign, there it was.

I had to appreciate Franc offering complimentary rides home for his revelers, but I was not about to leave them mid-way through the quests. "My choice is not up for debate, boys." I could almost feel the wave of protective male energy wash over me, but none of them pushed further. "Good. This feels like relationship growth."

Franc arched his brow, and he opened his mouth as if to reply, but Caden swept past him, cutting Franc off and sweeping me into his arms and off my feet. Caden grinned like a fool, his dimpled smile causing my heart to do flip-flops. "I'm glad you're staying because I can't wait to dance with you."

Marcos let out a low-toned growl as his panther-shifter eyes flashed green. Caden mock-pouted but set me back down gently. "This isn't some party, Caden. It's another of the fae's tricks. We can't even know what danger we're walking into."

The incubus shrugged off the panther-shifter's concerns. "I don't know about you guys, but even if it was the apocalypse, I'm not passing up an opportunity to dance."

Franc shook his head, a joyless laugh erupting from him. "How do you tell someone you're a demon without telling them you're a demon?"

I took a step toward the door, walking backwards as I pulled on Franc's burgundy suit sleeve. He held his ground, pursing his lips and pouting like I was the one being difficult. "You're overthinking this, Franc. Taneisha's sworn not to let anyone die and we're working great as a team. Let's keep a good thing going and get your legacy back, okay?"

Caden nodded in agreement, his gaze pinned to the sway of my hips. Everyone else was glowering at me.

I let go of Franc and crossed my arms. "Since when am I the fun one?"

Franc sighed. "You're usually the deliberate strategist

and I'd love the opportunity to meet 'rushes into fun headlong' Sera, but not when there's a fae pulling those strings."

I hated he had a point. Perhaps, having my powers back and swinging, I was just too eager to give them a whirl? I could admit to myself that they all had a point, but my heart was dead set on helping them. "I'm staying, Franc. I'm going to see this through until the end."

"Fine, if I can't talk you into heading home, at least we need to consider what we might walk into," Frank replied.

"Don't you and Marcos know this club inside and out?" I asked, looking back and forth between the two of them. "How hard will it be to search it from top to bottom?"

"It's big," Marcos replied, "with lots of twists and turns and a few notable detours. But you're right, we know it inside and out."

"We do not know who's in there," Franc added. "That's what worries me. Or how long they've been simmering."

I tapped a finger on my chin, muddling over his cooking analogy. "If this club were a gaming dungeon, I'd advise we go through it room by room, clearing out the bad guys and then searching for treasure."

That metaphor earned more than one arched brow from the guys.

"This is real life, not a game," Franc countered. "Those are real people in there. Perhaps my normal patrons, or perhaps creatures from some fae dimension. Maybe some of each. With Taneisha involved, we're guaranteed it won't be straightforward."

"Maybe not, but you were looking for a plan." I shrugged, but a sudden wave of unease washed over me.

"Wait, who are Velvet's typical patrons? Just people from around town, supes, visiting dignitaries, or what?"

He rocked his head from side to side. "We get all types. Mostly people from around town, but also a healthy mix of those in the supe communities."

"Oh," I replied, feeling my mouth form a little O as a panicked thought shot through my mind. I hadn't been seen in supe society or related events for some time, yet my family was well known. What if I ran into someone who knew me? Would they even recognize me? Would they care?

Or would I be called upon to wield my magic in public, just to fail spectacularly? I chewed on my bottom lip. "We can't know for sure from here. Let's slip inside and feel it out? Surely there's an entryway where we can peek around? Once we have the lay of the land, I can always go if we determine the situation is too dangerous," I offered. I knew I wouldn't be willing to leave later, but I wanted Franc to believe I was taking his concerns seriously.

Even if I wasn't entirely being honest. Or really at all. Who was I kidding? I wasn't about to leave them here.

Franc huffed out a sigh, the gleam in his eye letting me know he saw through my charade, but also appeared unwilling to fight me further on it. "Fine, but I'm kicking you out and shuttling you home at the first sign of danger."

I swayed my hips like I was ready to hit the dance floor. "Then let's check out the party."

AN EXPLOSIVE DISCOVERY

At first glance from just beyond the bouncer's pink velvet rope, Velvet looked like a typical club scene. Through the dim lights and fog machines, I gawked at the people who filled the dance floor. They moved in time to the music, but something about their movements left me with a sense of unease. I couldn't put my finger on why, but something was off. The beat was thrumming, beckoning me to bounce and grind to the rhythm. Liam had wrapped an arm around me as we'd walked into Velvet and now held me tight, no doubt worried I'd run off onto the dance floor if he let me go.

Of course, I wanted to go dance, which wasn't like me at all. I'd gotten used to living in the shadows of supe society, not living out loud where others might take notice of me.

I spied areas with tables and couches at the far end of the spacious room which were also covered with people, some bumping and grinding to their own not so private beats.

Oh my.

The reveler's behavior might not be discreet, but so far, this just looked like a hopping nightclub without a lot of rules. Then again, I had no benchmark to compare this to beyond my own assumptions.

Liam moved into a huddle with the posse, dragging me along with him. "What do you think?" Liam asked, his raised voice just barely carrying over the music.

Franc's expression was dark. "I don't recognize many of these people, but it's not as bad as I'd feared from what I can see here. Still, there's a feel to the club that's not quite right."

"Agreed. I'll do a quick round of recon," Marcos said. "Come with me?" he asked Liam.

Liam hesitated before glancing down at me protectively. Franc nodded to Liam before reaching out and pulling me close, passing me around like a delicate flower they didn't want to break. I wanted to hate their protective behavior, but I knew it wasn't because they thought of me as fragile. Even though I kept railing against their mating claims, a part of me thrilled every time their territorial natures surfaced.

With a glance back at me, Marcos and Liam disappeared into the crowd. Em and Caden crowded closer until I felt all three of them pressed up against me.

I tried not to think too long or too hard about what my feelings meant or where things might lead after the posse's quests finished. I reminded myself that right now we had bigger fish to fry, and I could worry about tomorrow, tomorrow.

"I normally adore Velvet," Em said. "But this crowd looks even more altered than usual."

Franc nodded. "I love a good ecstatic state, but this crowd looks downright glassy-eyed. Like they've been here soaking up the energy and going on for way too long."

"It's like they can't stop," I added.

"Ecstasy junkies," Em confirmed.

"Not everyone can drink from this energy well in moderation if left to their own devices. By its very nature, Dionysian magic has addictive properties. It's why I send some people away and why I close every morning. People need a break from their break, even if they don't realize it."

I nodded, even though I didn't fully understand what he meant. I knew Franc had said he wanted to bring me here to cut loose. It was clear these people had cut loose and then just kept going.

"Let me grab someone and see what we can find out," Em said. He slipped onto the dance floor and emerged a moment later with a sweat-soaked man who looked to be in his thirties in tow. The man's shaved head and his damp clothes clung to him like rags. His gaze was distant, and I wondered just how aware he was of his surroundings.

Franc stepped away from me and reached out to the man, running his hand down the side of his face. At his touch, the man's vision cleared, and he focused on Franc. His smile felt forced, and he panted, breathless and exhausted.

With Franc and Em focusing on the clubber, Caden moved behind me. The incubus wound his arms around my waist, planting a tender kiss on my shoulder. We swayed to the beat of the music, and I felt heat rising to my cheeks as I remembered the dream I had of us in the kitchen together. Images of Caden, his ice cream, and the feel of sugar-coated nuts pressed against my skin flooded my mind as I ground my hips back against Caden's crotch.

That had been a dream, right?

No wonder Franc wanted to bring me here. He'd said I needed to relax and let loose, and this club seemed to draw it out of me just by breathing the air and moving to the music.

"How long have you been here?" Franc asked the bald man.

The man's smile grew even wider as he threw his hands into the air. "No idea," he gasped. "An hour? A week? It doesn't matter, because this is the best party I've ever been to."

"I bet it is," Franc replied, not sounding like he'd taken the endorsement of his club as a compliment.

"I'm never going to leave." The man reached out and grabbed Franc's hand. "Come, join us," he begged. "Don't you want to dance? Can't you feel it bursting to get out?"

From the way Caden and I kept swaying back and forth to the beat, I thought I had an inkling of the call he was referring to. A languid energy was already seeping into my muscles and thoughts, easing my concerns as I gave myself over, bit by bit, to the rhythm.

"Come," said the bald man, looking at each of us as he gestured for us to come with him. "Can't you feel it calling you?"

At that moment, I glimpsed something glowing on the dance floor. Compelled by my curiosity, I slipped out of Caden's grasp and rushed forward past Franc, Em, and the bald man, determined to get a closer look.

"Shit!" Em's voice yelled out behind me. "Sera, Stop!"

"Keep up with her!" Franc shouted, his voice echoing across the dance floor.

I knew I wouldn't go far, but I couldn't stop. Compelled by a sudden curiosity, I didn't want to. I needed to know what I'd seen. I kept my eyes trained on the spot where I'd seen the glow, worried I'd lose track of the location if I let my gaze wander. I moved quickly, despite feeling unsteady in my high heels, as I threaded my way through the throng of moving people. Somehow, the path forward opened before me, almost as if choreographed by some higher power.

And then, as if fated, I found what I was hunting perched on a waist-high stand shaped like a short roman column. Encased in a cage-like basket of living vines stood a theater-style mask of a man's face crowned with clusters of grapes and leaves. Magic pulsed from the mask, undulating in waves outward, no doubt the reason behind the crowd's enchantment. My magic sparkled around my fingertips, vibrating beneath my skin, as if in response to the thrumming beat or the ripples of magic rolling off the mask, or both.

Franc's mask! It had to be!

"Taneisha didn't even make this one hard to find," I muttered to myself, aware no one appeared to be paying attention to me. Triumphant in my find, I reached out and pulled at the living mesh of vines, determined to free the mask. The moment my hands grasped the cage, the music stopped, and I could have sworn I was falling forward despite my eyes reassuring me I wasn't moving at all. My magic poured into the vines, twisting along their weaving pattern like water sucked into desert sand. My hands burned with an invisible fire as a raw, electric jolt of pure power erupted from my flesh. The vines shone with a bright pink light ribboned through with the utter blackness of void space, crackling and spitting with an unearthly sound.

I stood stock still, unable to move. To do anything. My hands burned, locked in place against the cage of chaotic magic. The music returned louder than before, almost as if the bass was trying to pound itself into my bones.

"Sera!" I heard Em's voice behind me. "Get away from…" he commanded, but it was too late.

Propelled by a blast wave from my wild magic, I flew backwards and landed on someone. Maybe multiple someones? My body felt limp. Drained. Were my eyes open, because everything was black?

"I've got you," Em's voice came from somewhere around me, but he sounded oh so far away. The music had suddenly faded, and I heard distant-sounding screams.

"Dammit, woman," Caden's voice floated somewhere above me. I heard movement but couldn't quite track what was happening. "Is she breathing?"

I had the sense that people were touching me, but the sensations were the faintest of faint, like they were coming from another place entirely.

"She's not," Em replied, his voice sounding strained. "Help me get her on her back," he said.

"Hurry, Em," Caden pleaded.

"What the hell happened?" Franc demanded. "She was only gone a moment." I tried to imagine the expression that accompanied his tone. I could sense a lecture coming.

Instead of an answer to Franc's question, a warmth flooded through my body. Where I'd felt distant, sensation rushed through me, pinpricks of pain quickly replaced by an awareness flooding through my aching body. Lips covered my own as life force poured into me. I opened my eyes to find a relieved-looking Emrys staring down at me, his dark-brown eyes locked on mine.

I coughed once, then twice, but he continued to hover over me as his healing magic coursed through my veins. When he stopped and then pulled back, I coughed again, a sparkling glitter of golden energy wafting around me and hung in the air between us.

"You know how to show a girl a good time," I said to Em, my voice hoarse and my throat dry as the desert.

The corner of his mouth hitched. "You're impossible, mage. And if you think I'll let you get away before I can show you an actual good time, well..." Em's tone was flippant, but the look in his eyes was something else. Fear? Anger? I didn't quite have my wits about me to know.

The weight of what had just happened hit me like a ton of bricks. I'd known Emrys, a demi-god of Isis, had the power of resurrection in his back pocket, but I'd never seen his magic in action before. I did not know what it had cost him to help me, but I knew I owed him, now and forever.

"Resurrecting a gal to prove a point?" I joked, but from the looks on Em's, Franc's, and Caden's faces, I wasn't at all funny. I held my hands to my face, remembering how my magic combined with the cage of vine had seared my flesh. My palms were red and sore, but somehow intact.

"Can you sit up?" Em asked, holding out his hand, and I nodded. Caden was on the other side of me, and together they helped me sit up. Considering I hadn't been breathing a moment ago, now I felt energized. Ready to boogie, even. But Em pulled me close, scooping me up against his body and then standing up, cradling me against him the entire time.

"Let me help," Caden offered.

Em stepped back, pulling me away from Caden. "You let her run straight into danger a few minutes ago, so I don't think so."

"Have you tried stopping Sera from doing what she wants to do?" Caden replied, for once sounding like the voice of reason.

"I found Franc's mask," I pointed out, triumphant despite my near-death experience. "I'm the winner."

"We see you did," Franc replied. I followed his gaze over to the cage encircling his divine mask. Instead of vines, it now pulsed with a bright, neon pink light.

"That can't be good," I muttered, only then taking a better look around at the now deserted space. Where a few moments ago it'd been full of dancers and hip music, the music had faded and the main room was now deserted except for a few people passed out or sleeping on the couches dotting the edges of the space. "Where the hell did everyone go?"

"It's a big club," Franc answered. "When you sent chaos magic flying in all directions, the revelers fled to other areas."

"Huh," was all I could come up with. Just how big was this place? Despite the relative quiet in the club, I sensed a tense but energetic buzz in the air. It was like we were all waiting for something to happen, but what?

"Indeed," Franc replied, his tone terse as his attention flipped back to the caged mask. "Obviously finding the mask wasn't the challenge."

Marcos and Liam strode in through a different direction than they'd left, neither looking at all okay with the situation. My fingers itched to touch them, like a hunger ran just under my flesh. I slipped out of Em's arms, at once missing the feel of him against me. When I reached out and touched both shifters' chests, a soothing calm rolled over me. Liam and Marcos exchanged glances as they responded to my touch, Liam running a hand down my arm, and Marcos placing his steadying hand protectively around my hip.

"There are people everywhere and some expanded spaces," Marcos informed us. "What the hells happened in here?"

Liam, eyes locking on the caged mask, let out a low whistle. "That looks like an answer wrapped in a problem."

"You have no idea," Franc answered, watching us with questions in his eyes. "Wait, what do you mean by 'expanded spaces'?"

"I'll have to show you," Marcos replied, gesturing for us to follow him.

We turned to go, and Em snatched me from the shifters, scooping me up into his arms. I craved his touch too, so didn't complain, letting him draw me in close. I couldn't deny how his alpha moves revved me up, and neither could my magic, which crackled noisily along my fingertips. If my magic hurt Em, he didn't show it.

I wiggled against Em, loving the way his fingers dug into my thighs. "Can you let me go? I can walk fine."

"No," he answered, turning on his heel and heading for the front of the club.

"What are you doing?" I asked.

"I'm sending you home while we work this mess out," Em replied.

"You can't do that," I said, panicking over the prospect of being away from the posse. "You'll need my help to detangle the chaos magic."

"I agree with Em," Franc called after us. "We'll find another way after Sera's safe and away from here."

"No," I looked back and forth between the two of them, but it was clear they'd made up their minds. "No, you can't just ship me back home." My pleas were falling on deaf ears, but with each step Em took away from the others, the magic leaking from my hands flared more brightly. "Marcos! Liam! Caden!" I called out, but they'd all fallen in line with Em and Franc, leaving me no way around their decision.

Em rounded the pink rope, nearing the wide-open front doors of the club. "None of us will risk your death for our legacies."

My vision blurred as hot, heavy tears ran down my cheeks. He couldn't do this. I needed to be here. "So, you're just kicking me to the curb?"

Before I knew what was happening, Em lowered me to my feet and pinned me to the wall, his lips once again capturing my own with an intensity that rivaled the heat of the sun. But instead of filling me with the breath of life, this time he stole my breath away.

I almost forgot what we'd been fighting over, but then he backed away, slipped his arm around my waist, and headed us straight out the door. Impossibly, we smashed into an invisible barrier, knocking us backwards and sending sparks of my magic shooting out from my hands, lighting up the space around us like a holiday light display.

Caden, who'd been following close on our heels, caught us both before we fell over.

"Ow!" I exclaimed, leaning against Caden as I rubbed my knee and elbow where I'd hit the invisible wall. "So much for sending me home." Magic pooled in my gut and shimmered around my hands in response to my growing frustration.

Emrys tested the barrier, touching at first, and then pounding his fist against it. Caden was next, to no avail. Franc edged past them, testing out the barrier himself.

"Damn," Franc said. "At least now we know why there are so many people in the club. No one can leave."

"Wrong. There's still one way we can get Sera out of danger," Em said. "Taneisha, Taneisha, Taneisha!"

AN UNPRECEDENTED APOLOGY

FRANC

I fumed at Emrys for invoking the vengeful fae. Not that I disagreed with his instinct to keep Sera safe, but that he'd done it without consulting the rest of the posse. Our teamwork had flown out the window when we'd arrived at Velvet, and we'd need to rally in order to win my mask back. Of that, I was certain.

This quest just kept getting better and better. And by better, I meant crappier. I'd been eager to get my legacy back, but now that we were here, in Velvet, I wish I'd tried harder to foil Taneisha before she'd fouled my club. A shiver went down my spine thinking of the new club areas Marcos had mentioned. Velvet was perfect. At least it had been. What awful fae expansions did I have waiting for me to clean up?

Taneisha messing with Velvet crossed a line. Fucking with my livelihood, my divine mission, and my raison d'être, went beyond the pale. The fae would pay. I added her transgression to my mental ledger, took a deep breath, and then shifted gears. Now was the time to solve the problem at hand, not plan my retribution.

There'd be time for that later, after we'd won back all our legacies.

When Taneisha materialized next to my caged mask on that pedestal, my anger flared despite my best intentions. I tamped down my reaction and held my tongue. The last thing I needed to do right now was goad her into making things worse for us.

"Well, hello, bacchants!" Taneisha exclaimed. "I trust you're enjoying the party?"

To my surprise, the fae was still wearing that simple black jumpsuit. This stood out to me as every time we'd seen her previously, she'd shown up rocking a different outfit. Was she losing her edge or busy with something else?

"We're..." I started, but then Emrys stormed up to the fae, side stepping around me and getting right up into her face.

"Send Sera home. Now," he demanded.

Taneisha's ever smug smile faltered. She craned her neck around Emrys, taking in the rest of us, and then she gazed around the club. When she looked down at the caged mask beside her, her jaw dropped in shock.

"Who the hell slapped a geas on my box?"

Not exactly the type of confidence-boosting reaction you hoped for from your scheming captor.

Sera sashayed up, arms crossed, a spray of chaotic magic trailing her steps across the black floor. I couldn't help but appreciate the way those stilettos highlighted her long legs or how that wisp of a dress shimmered down her curves as she moved. I also didn't miss the electric sparks dancing around her fingertips or the matching fiery look in her eyes.

"I tried to rip apart the vines to remove the mask, but something happened with my magic and, well, that happened." She gestured to the vines that her pink energy had transformed, sending sparks flying. "It threw me off of it and we haven't tried it again yet."

"How peculiar," Taneisha muttered. "That's all you did?" The fae looked at Sera like she'd never seen her before, and I wondered if the fae was out of her depth with this challenge.

Just my luck.

"You're leaving out the part where you stopped breathing, and I had to revive you," Emrys added. "We tried to take Sera outside to call a ride, but you've locked us all in."

"I couldn't have you abandoning your quest, could I?" Taneisha looked around for a response, but then thought better of it. "Still, you shouldn't have been able to geas my knot," she said to Sera, who just shrugged back at her. "Your magic is indeed curiouser than I realized. Almost reckless, even. Now, I said I'd send you home and I am a fae of my word."

"Only because you're magically bound to do so," I added.

Taneisha ignored me and held out a hand to Sera. "Be that as it may, shall we go?"

Sera pursed her lips, then glanced around at the posse, a hunger burning in her eyes. She shook her head. "I'm not leaving until we get the mask."

"Don't be ridiculous," Emrys pleaded with Sera. "You could have died."

Sera cupped Emrys' cheek in her hand, her magic seeming to calm down at their brief touch. Interesting. "I didn't die because you brought me back. We're a team and I'm not about to cut out on you."

"It's not quitting when we give you permission," I said. I didn't want Sera to go, but if she did, it might be for the best, especially with her magic so volatile. The posse might work better without her presence as a constant distraction. Then again, her absence might drive Liam and Marcos' shifter natures crazy.

I wasn't sure which option was better, and I was half inclined to push for her to stay just so we could keep an eye on her.

"I'm not changing my mind," Sera replied. "I'm in this to the end."

Taneisha had been watching our exchange, a frown on her face all the while. For once she didn't appear smug, and I wondered what could have knocked her back down to earth.

"In that case," Taneisha began, "let me apologize for this quest getting sidelined."

I didn't know how to react to a fae apologizing. What had come over Taneisha? By the stunned looks on the other's faces, they shared my confusion.

Taneisha watched us for a reaction, and when it didn't come, continued. "Let me explain a little more about your challenge. This," she pointed to the box, taking care not to touch the glowing pink cords, "is an entanglement knot." She looked at me, waiting expectantly.

"Let me guess. It's an unsolvable knot which only the smartest can solve," I explained. "You've designed it to be impossible."

"I knew you'd recognize this challenge," she replied, flashing me a potentially genuine smile. "Franc is the one who needs to untangle it, because it's his legacy inside. However, you need to wait until Sera's magic geas diffuses. I don't recommend touching it again until the pink glow fades."

Sera arched her brow. "I don't get why you're being extra nice, Taneisha, or throwing us extra clues. Is this some new level of mind games?"

Taneisha's jaw dropped. "No, I swear it's not," she argued earnestly. "I just feel bad that things went wrong with the knot. It's truly not what I'd intended." [1]

Now we had not just one, but two apologies. Sera and I exchanged a glance, while Emrys just stood all up in Taneisha's space, glowering at her.

Taneisha held up her hands. "Look, I need to do a little research to figure out how to undo the geas she added to my magic. I'll try not to be too long. In the meantime, if you can find a way for Sera to burn off some of her magic safely, perhaps it'll help drain off the geas?"

"You're playing mighty genuine, T," I said. "But I believe actions, not words."

"She's stringing us along," Emrys said. "You should try unraveling the knot now."

Taneisha had the gall to look shocked. "There's no need to be rude, Emrys. And Franc, I would really not take his advice lest you be the next one to get kicked out of your body. Look, I'll be back as soon as I can." She winked at me and poofed away without another word.

A moment of silence descended as we circled up around the glowing, caged mask.

"That was weird as fuck," Liam said, saying what we all felt. "What do we think?"

"She's obviously lying," Emrys said. "We have to assume everything she said was just to lead us astray."

"Fae can't lie," Marcos replied. "But you're right, they'll mislead as far as they're able. We can't trust anything she says."

Sera drifted up against Caden, leaning against him as his arm curled around her waist. She leaned her head back against his shoulder and sighed as he buried his nose in her hair. "I almost get the impression that something's wrong with her," Sera added.

"Do we care?" I replied.

Sera shrugged. "It might give us leverage. If I get the opportunity, I'll see if I can drag more information out of her."

Caden looked up. "That's fair. What's clear is Taneisha expects us to stay awhile and look around."

"Not like she's made leaving an option," Liam added. "But we can't mess with the geas on the entanglement knot safely yet, so what are our other options?"

"We could test the knot and see if it's actually dangerous," Marcos said. "But I'm not volunteering to be our guinea pig."

"You're not either," Emrys said, pointing to Sera.

Sera mocked surprise, shaking her head. "Me? Never? Besides, I already did."

It earned her a round of glowering from all of us.

Caden ran a hand through Sera's hair, brushing it out of his face. "I have to admit, I'm curious about what we'll find. I say we explore."

"The possibilities are turning my stomach," I said. "I

hate to think of what I'll have to clean up after all of this is over."

"I'm game to find something to blow up and burn off some steam," Sera added. From the way her magic was dripping off her fingertips and floating around as little ashy embers, I assumed she meant it literally.

"No," I snapped, pointing my index finger at her in warning. "No explosions, fires, or knocking down walls in Velvet. I forbid it."

Sera answered me with a slight, sultry smile as she held up her hand as if taking an oath. "Find me another option and I'll be good. I swear it."

I wished I could believe her, but her words dripped with sarcasm. I couldn't wait to teach her a lesson she wouldn't forget.

"So, we're off to burn off some of Sera's magic?" Liam asked, an eager glint in his eyes as he eyed Sera.

"No actual burning," I added. "Metaphorical burning only. Emphasis on energy burn."

"Fine. Energy draining only," Caden confirmed.

"Let's have a look around," Sera replied. She sauntered around the circle, her hips swinging as that shimmering, beaded fabric rolled from side to side across her skin as she came to lean against me. "I seem to remember you promising to show me around Velvet?"

"Happy to." I offered her my arm, which she slid hers over, a frisson of anticipation passing between us. I hooked my fingers under her chin, lifting her face to meet my ravenous gaze. "At least with you beside me, I can keep you out of trouble."

Sera shivered against me, her gaze flitting back between my eyes and my lips. When she spoke, her tone was breathy. "You keep telling yourself that, Franc, but I'm not the demi-god of madness here. This is your mad house, after all."

"Touché," I grinned down at her. I brushed my thumb over her plump lips, trailing my fingers across her jawline and then down her neck. A trail of sparks followed my touch, a sign of just how close Sera's magic was to erupting. She shivered under my touch, and a smile broke out across my lips as I thought of the rooms I planned to show her. "Although I like to think of Velvet as less of a mad-house and more of a den of iniquity."

Sera's eyes lit up, and she let out a low chuckle. "If you say so. I swear I'm pulling on my best possibility mindset. Now, show me your vision of inspiration."

Sera was going to be the death of me. I just hoped my club survived my quest and Sera's overflowing chaos energy.

---

1. Wondering why Taneisha had a change of heart? Check out the bonus epilogue to Hidden Hearts to learn more! https://geni.us/ HiddenHeartsBonus

MISSING PERSONS

FRANC

I led the posse off the dance floor and past the bar, pausing at an archway leading outside. Many of the people who'd scattered earlier had fled to the outside garden and were now milling about like hesitant children in unfamiliar territory.

Sera's earlier display had nearly panicked me, and Velvet had responded in kind by muting the music and turning up the house lights. The building wasn't exactly sentient, but I'd poured so much of myself into it so that in many ways, it functioned as an extension of my wants and desires.

Which was the very reason Taneisha's machinations worried me. My club wasn't just empty space you could tack on extra rooms to and have it all function seamlessly. Sera was correct in saying my magic held the edge of madness within it. Any changes to Velvet would change the way my magic ebbed and flowed within these walls. I doubted Taneisha had taken any of my club's unique construction into account.

I willed it to be so, and the music returned to the dance floor with a heavy beat as the house lights dimmed. Like an invocation, the partiers in the garden perked up and started filtering back into the main hall, eager for the high they could only reach through the combined pounding of the beats and their feet in unison.

I led us outside, easily ducking out of the way of the returning throng. While most of the posse let me stay in the lead, Marcos came to the fore, standing on the other side of Sera. Em, Caden, and Liam lagged us, chatting amongst themselves. Although I was curious about what they were discussing, I was content with keeping my focus on Sera.

"It doesn't appear that Taneisha altered the gardens," Marcos said. "But we should inspect them before heading to the temple."

Sera looked at me askance. "You have a religious space in your club?"

I chuckled, trying to think of how a newbie like Sera might experience Velvet for the first time. "All acts of love and pleasure are forms of worship. My temple is a multi-use, polytheistic space. Velvet has several adjoining spaces designed to further a person's separation from their ego, each on a different level."

"Oh," she replied, her mouth forming a small o. She pressed herself closer to me, and I wondered just how conscious she was of her current behavior. "Well, I hadn't expected a garden either."

Yeah, mon chéri, take that and noodle it about in that overthinking mind of yours for a few minutes.

Then Marcos' earlier statement caught up with me,

causing fingers of dread to claw at my chest. "Wait, don't tell me the fae altered my temple?"

"I don't mean to worry you, but yes, somewhat."

I thought of a million and one epithets to add to Taneisha's name. Befouler? Rotter? Taint? Not that I'd list any out loud. With my luck, she'd hear me and make things worse for us. I shook my head. Perhaps the damage wasn't that bad? I'd need to see for myself before I could even know what it would take to fix whatever she'd changed.

I'd never find out standing here. By now, the crowds had thinned, as many had returned to the dance floor.

"Ow!" Sera cried out, doubling over as a wave of heat rolled off of her. Marcos and I steadied Sera as sparks ran through her ebony tresses and rolled down off her shoulders. A pair of clubbers walked past us, pointing at Sera and her magical display.

Whether or not they were supes, the last thing Sera needed was people noticing her erratic magic.

"Let's get moving," I said, meeting Marcos' concerned gaze. We had to get Sera to a secluded space where she could melt down without her magic being exposed, and my temple was the perfect spot.

"Tell me more about this garden," Sera prompted, looking up at me out of anxious eyes, leaning heavily against me as she tread carefully on the concrete in her heels. "I can use the distraction."

We trekked through the gardens, which were dotted with traditional stone sculptures of graceful creatures, tall, thin cypress trees, and benches. I led us around the crowd, partly so I could see the gardens with my own eyes and know they were okay, and partly to shield Sera from view.

The gardens were one of my favorite areas of Velvet, even if it was the tamest. Sera seemed content to let me lead her around and play tour guide, which was a fresh development from her typical headstrong attitude. Perhaps the accident with the knot had taken more out of her than she was admitting? Worry for her gnawed at me, despite knowing just how capable a woman she was.

"The central garden acts as a physical and mental courtyard between the other spaces," I explained, happy to distract her. "It allows patrons a temporary break from the intensity of the experience and gives an opportunity to cool off and chat with other like-minded types."

"But everyone enters via the dance club?"

"Usually. There are separate entrances for elite members to certain private areas, but yes, that's the main entrance."

"So, there might be other exits we could use?"

"We'll check as we go," Marcos said, "but I'd assume Taneisha magically blocked all of them."

"Talk about a fire code violation," Sera quipped.

We rounded a line of cypress, coming face to face with a trio of faces which were not regulars to Velvet.

Sera started, clearly not expecting to run into them. She pulled away from me, took a step away, and clasped her hands behind her back, obviously working to hide her out of control magic, and her intimate relationship with me, from their view. It was of little use, however, as even with her hands hidden behind her back, the pulsating pinkish glow lit up the ground behind her.

From the sudden shift in Sera's mood, I half expected her to take off, but perhaps she wasn't feeling that steady on her feet. I turned my attention to new arrivals, wondering what about these men had our mage so off-kilter.

"Hey, I thought I recognized you, cousin," said the black-haired man of slight build.

"Hey, back," was all Sera said in reply, nibbling on her lower lip. She cast a worried glance at the tall blonde man, so of course I wondered who he was, or had been, to her.

The two men wore tailored suits ready for a night about town. A curvy woman in a black long-sleeved dress hung off the arm of the man who'd greeted Sera. He eyed us with peaked interest. Unlike the bald man we'd talked to earlier, these people appeared mentally alert. I guessed they were recent arrivals, and thus not yet overcome with the fae's magic.

The tall, broad shouldered blonde man didn't say a word, instead cast a brooding look at Sera in a way that instinctively had me wanting to knock him down a notch. I suspected there was some history between them, but as long as he behaved himself, I'd leave well enough alone. After all, we had bigger and more fae fish to fry at the moment.

Em, Caden, and Liam emerged from around the trees behind us, and wordlessly stepped up into something of a semi-circle surrounding Sera. It wasn't exactly a threatening posture, but it wasn't exactly not, either.

Beyond Sera's simple greeting, our mage stood still as a deer in the headlights, as if she were waiting for divine intervention to save her from the inevitable impact. I recalled Sera sharing her history about living in isolation from the supe community and figured she was worried about what they might tell her family.

Surrounded by us, surely she knew she had nothing to

fear from these other supes? Not with the posse by her side. But Taneisha had proven to us with her illusions that she'd go to great lengths to mess with our heads, so we needed to play along and figure out this puzzle. That meant figuring out what part these newcomers might play into the fae's game.

Someone had to break the tension, so I stepped forward, placing myself between the newcomers and Sera. "I'm Franc Lyaeus. And you are?"

The black-haired man's eyes lit up in recognition of my name, and he dipped his chin out of respect. "This is your club."

I inclined my head. At least this one knew who was in charge. "It is, although I admit it's seen better days."

He smiled widely, as if I'd made some sort of private joke. "I'm Mikael Stagsky. This is my companion Ella Asherah, and my friend Chadwick Macheret. We were looking for a way out. Do you know the way?"

His question confirmed my fears. Taneisha hadn't only locked us in here. Anyone else who wandered in would be stuck until we completed our quest. I assumed as Mikael called Sera his cousin, that meant he too was a mage. Perhaps, despite Sera's obvious anxiety, these three could be useful to us.

"Sadly, no. It appears there's some sort of magical barrier preventing our exit. How long have you been here?" I asked, leaving out the obvious question of who'd caused the barrier.

This time Chadwick answered. "It's been some hours since we arrived. Maybe even overnight? Time flows differently since we got here, plus our phones and watches don't seem to work anymore. Do you know what's going on?"

His attitude rubbed me the wrong way, despite his question being reasonable.

"Unfortunately, you're caught along with us in a fae's vengeful trap. She's deluded and trying to teach me a lesson, careless about who else might get caught up in the crossfire. Most likely, we're all stuck here until I can free my mask, which you might have noticed on the dance floor."

"We need to step up our time frame," Marcos whispered in my direction. "We can't draw this out over a couple of days like the prior quests without endangering the people stuck in here."

"Have you been stuck in here all week?" Mikael asked Sera, the concern in his eyes genuine.

There was that deer in the headlights stare from Sera again, and her magic glowed even more brightly. "What do you mean?" she asked, her voice climbing an octave.

"I heard from mom about a week ago that you'd gone missing. She said Dara Lowe put out a missing mage report saying you'd disappeared and might have even been abducted." Mikael frowned, glancing at each of us.

I assumed Ms. Lowe was family because of the shared name, but admittedly, I didn't understand the inner workings of mage hierarchy or Sera's lineage in that detail. Mikael was right to suspect we caused Sera's extended absence, not that I'd be confirming it for him.

"Abducted?" Sera let out a nervous laugh, rolling her eyes. She moved to tuck her hair behind her ear, magic falling from her hands like she was holding sparklers, but she ignored it like it wasn't even happening. "What nonsense. Aunt Sophie is such a lovely person, I know she means well. Please give your mother my regards," Sera replied. "I assure you there's nothing to be concerned about. I just forgot to tell everyone I'd be away for a few days at this semi-spontaneous job. Whoops?"

Mages were known for their smooth-talking diplomacy but seeing Sera so off balance and chittering like a nervous chipmunk was a surprise. She moved her hands back behind her back, but the glow of the magic continued to grow, with the occasional ember catching in the breeze.

The three shared dubious glances. Chadwick cocked his head to the side, his expression doubtful. "You took a job with the owner of Velvet and his... friends?"

They weren't buying Sera's story, and I didn't blame them. Considering someone had reported her missing, I would have been suspicious in their shoes, too.

Sera's smile turned wooden, and she shrugged, as this wasn't anything important. As if we weren't anything important. "Yeah. We know each other from my days at Goldenbriar Academy. When they offered me this job, I felt I had to help them out. I must have forgotten to log my plans with the mage guild."

Mikael's brow arched. "So, this is just a job?"

Sera tossed her hair again. "Exactly. Just a job."

I clenched my jaw so hard I also expected to hear a tooth crack. Did Sera really just minimize all of us, as if nothing we'd been through meant anything? Liam let out a low growl, and Caden's usual smirk was sour. My irritation rolled around my gut like a living thing, and it took all my focus to hold my tongue. It's not like I, or any of us, could claim her. Sera had allowed none of us to claim her, but now that she was publicly denying us, all I wanted to do was prove to her how wrong she was.

Sera needed us. Wanted us. Even if she couldn't admit it to herself.

Ella pulled away from Mikael and sidestepped around me. "Are you sure you're alright?" she asked Sera, her soothing, melodic voice at odds with the slight frown pulling down the corners of her deep red lips.

Sera nodded a bit too eagerly. "I'm totally fine." A breeze swept through, sweeping Sera's hair across her face. She absentmindedly raised her hand, which was still sparkling with red and pink embers, and tucked her hair behind her ear.

The casual, and now repeated, display of magic didn't go unnoticed. Mikael's brows shot up, and he and Chadwick shared a look of concern. Everyone's focus shifted to Sera's hand, which she tucked behind her back, hiding them away from Mikael, Ella, and Chadwick.

Sera looked down at her hands, finally seeming to understand that everyone could see her lack of control over her magic. I knew she was worried about her family and other mages discovering how chaotic her magic would be. Now there was no denying it. Unless we could manage these three and somehow convince them to keep Sera's secret, that fear would become a reality.

"You don't look fine," Ella replied. "I could soothe you," she offered, holding up her hand.

"You're a siren?" I asked Ella. With her siren's gifts, Ella no doubt was reading us like a book. Forget about letting Sera's magic secret out of the bag. How would she feel about whatever this was between all of us being revealed? I couldn't imagine Sera would welcome that, especially when she wasn't even willing to claim us as her own.

Ella nodded, the brilliant green of her eyes fixing on me. "I am, and I'm happy to help calm the mage. It seems she could use my help."

"Sera's fine," Em said, pulling Sera behind him and moving between her and Ella. "We've got her covered."

Ella's eyes widened as a beat of silence passed between all of us. A look of understanding passed over Ella's face as she looked back and forth between us, and I knew that the siren innately understood our dynamic, perhaps even better than we did. Ella held up her hands in mock surrender and stepped back beside Mikael. "I meant no overstep."

"None taken, Ella. It's been a long day for all of us," I replied. How ironic was it that the siren could read the room, yet Sera remained in denial over us being her mates?

"Where did you say you've been this past week on this so-called job?" Chadwick asked, his expression full of contempt, glancing between Sera and the rest of us. "And what's going on with your magic?"

"Neither of those is any of your business," Sera snapped back, planting her still-glowing hands on her hips. Veins of raw magical power erupted under her feet as she spoke, but Sera appeared not to notice. The lines invaded the cement and grass in a series of growths, all aimed directly at Chadwick. I was torn between feeling relieved that she wasn't worried about her friends seeing her wielding magic and worried that she was about to further lose control. "I said I'm fine, Chad," she said, saying his name like an insult, "and frankly, we've got bigger things to worry about right now than my social calendar."

Mikael and I shared a look, his gaze glancing to the wild magic beneath Sera and then back to me. His arched brow seemed to ask, 'are you going to handle this?' and I gave the slightest of nods, and he wordlessly pursed his lips in reply. Sera's magical reaction had slowed, but the posse needed to help her curb her chaos, and quickly.

Anger flashed in Chadwick's eyes as he readied for a retort, but Ella placed a hand on his arm, and he immediately calmed under her siren's influence.

"Fair enough," Mikael replied. "Does this job involve freeing us from the fae's lockdown on Velvet?"

"It does," I said. "We could use your help, if you're willing?"

Mikael nodded. "What can we do?"

"Back at the main dance floor, there were several people overcome with exhaustion and substances," I explained. "Perhaps Ella's gifts would be helpful there?"

"Definitely. I'll be happy to level out anyone who needs it," Ella replied.

"What else?" Mikael asked.

"I don't know your powers, but are you able you use your gifts to check for hidden magic and exits?" Marcos asked. "Just avoid the caged mask in the center of the dance floor. Only Franc can touch it. If you can look around the pool area, that'd be great."

"Pool?" I asked. "Velvet doesn't have a pool."

"It does now," Liam said, and I just shook my head in disdain. "It's the new first right after leaving the dance club."

"Okay, we can check there. How will we find you?" Ella asked.

"We're headed to the temple, but let's plan to meet back here in the central garden in, say, about an hour?" I asked.

"That long? What will you be doing in the temple?" Chadwick asked, not bothering to hide the sneer on his face.

This guy needed an attitude check.

"Whatever it takes to win against the fae's games," I answered without hesitation.

"Good luck," Mikael said, turning to go with Ella at his side. He pushed Chadwick's shoulder, who grudgingly followed along, but not before casting a moody look back in Sera's direction.

I stepped close to Sera, slid my arm around her waist, and then steered her to walk with me. The others followed. Marcos was glowering, although I didn't know about what.

"What's up with that Chad asshole?" Caden asked once they were out of earshot.

"Ugh," Sera said, running her fingers roughly through her hair. "Chad's an ex-boyfriend. I broke things off with him when my magic went wild to hide things. Not that it matters now."

As a group, we quieted. I hadn't quite been sure what the dynamic was between Chad and Sera, but I suppose I should have.

"Dibs on flattening Chad the next time we see him," Caden said.

"If I don't get to him first," Em added.

Sera barked out a laugh. "You don't have to go all macho alpha on me. I can kick his ass myself whenever I want to." She swirled her finger through the air to demonstrate, leaving a trail of electric sparkles in its wake.

"We don't have to, my dear," I said, whispering into her ear. "But we will 'go alpha' on you whenever we feel it's needed."

Sera rolled her eyes, but she leaned into me as if she couldn't help but deepen the contact between us. "Assuming I let you," she murmured.

"Oh, my dear, you won't just let us," I taunted. She looked up at me, her lower lip caught between her teeth. "You'll beg us."

THE TEMPLE OF DIONYSOS

MARCOS

The sultry, ambient music of the temple hit me before we even crossed under the archway. Vines clung to the decorative stonework of the arch, with the words, "The art of living well and the art of dying well are one," carved into the gray granite surface. I'd read that phrase over and over, but never had it hit me in the gut like it did today after days and days of Taneisha putting us all at risk.

Placing my mate, our mate, at risk.

I tensed, grinding my teeth, as I crossed over the threshold, the magic in this space rolling over my skin like an old friend's embrace. For anyone else, the energy here would loosen their inhibitions and free their mind, but I'd long since acclimated to my near daily exposure to it. We walked into the entryway, the sounds of devotees emanating from the other side of the curtain which separated the temple space proper from passers-by.

Sera wobbled on her feet, clinging to Franc's arm for support. "Woah, what was that?"

"Each space in the club has a unique feel," Franc replied, running his fingers down Sera's arm. "The magic within the temple has a way of breaking down boundaries, freeing our more animalistic natures."

Liam leaned in close. "You look uncomfortable," Liam whispered, a sly smile playing across his lips. There was an ease in his movements that hadn't been there a moment ago, and a glint of humor in his eyes. "Which is weird, considering the magic here exists to release inhibitions."

I shrugged it off. "I've worked at Velvet for so long the magic doesn't hit me the same way. I'm not sure if it's Franc giving me a pass or the club itself recognizing that I'm here to protect it and the people inside."

Liam's smile faltered at the note of caution in my words, and he looked back out over the crowd, as if he could find whatever was unsettling me.

Franc arched a brow at me, making out our conversation despite our quiet voices. "Maybe it's both?"

"You're telling me you don't know?" I shook my head. My panther ached to get out and pace, but I held him in check. Franc just shrugged. I didn't believe he didn't know. He controlled every aspect of the magic in Velvet, so he had to know. Then again, maybe he didn't know this time around with Taneisha messing with the club.

That thought didn't help settle my nerves one bit.

Caden walked up to the black curtain and poked his head inside. "Maybe you're just dull, Marcos?" he jibed, not even looking back at me before letting out a low whistle. "Shit, it's a lively crowd tonight."

"A hungry crowd." Liam's wolfish voice spoke directly into my thoughts.

His words rang true, a sense of disquiet lingering in my gut, knowing he might pick up on the same thing.

"It's all perfect," Franc purred. He stepped away from Sera and grabbed one of the charm necklaces off the wall. "You'll be needing this," he said, sliding it over her head and adjusting the sliding knots along the cord to keep the amulet close to her neck.

Sera touched the bronzed ivy leaf charm hanging at her throat. "What's this for?"

"It's Velvet's solution for birth control," I explained. "With that on you don't have to worry about pregnancy or STDs."

Sera's cheeks flushed an alluring shade of rose that I would never tire of seeing. "Oh..."

"She doesn't need to worry about diseases with us anyway," Caden drawled, his heated gaze passing over each of us. By the red glow in his eyes, Caden's incubi nature was right at home in the temple. "We supes are impervious."

Only Caden could reference sexually transmitted diseases and make it sound sexy.

"So wait, we're here in the temple to..." Sera's words slipped away as her fingers touched the charm around her neck.

"Sex, Sera. And lots of it," Franc answered. Sera's brows shot up. "Taneisha said we needed to burn off some of your magic, and this seems like a safe and pleasurable way to wear you out. Do you disagree?"

Sera's tongue snaked out, licking those luscious lips of hers. "I mean, I'm a fan of sex, especially sex with all of you. But I'm not sure how wise it is to follow the advice of a fae?"

"The lady has a point." Liam's words filled my mind.

"You've got a better idea?" I asked.

Liam shook his head.

Franc held his hands out, motioning for us all to chill out. "Trust me," he said, striding past the curtain like the ringmaster he was, confident we'd follow.

Liam and Caden followed close behind Franc, while Sera leaned against me, threading her arm through mine for support. My panther purred with pride, earning a knowing glance from Liam, who had picked up on his reaction. My neck prickled, and I glanced back at Emrys, who stood with his arms crossed and his glower pointed right at me.

"What?" I asked him.

Emrys frowned, but then shrugged. "Nothing."

What the hells? I didn't have the energy to drag details out of his cranky ass. "Fine, stew away." I brushed off his bad mood and smiled down at Sera, who I'd safely tucked against me. "C'mon, gorgeous."

Sera's smile dazzled me. I knew my reaction to Sera was partly just Velvet's energy, but I liked to think I'd always be soft for her, my mate, like this.

We followed Franc's path into the temple, which was packed with revelers. I watched Sera's reaction to the wild scene unfolding around us. The walls vibrated with sensual energy, and people lost to seeking pleasure in more ways than I could count. Right in front of us were a cuddle of bodies lounging and giggling to themselves on a pedestal of a bed, all of them in different stages of undress.

"Oh. Wow," Sera gasped. "Just wow."

"Just another evening in the temple," I replied.

"Wait, are we supposed to jump in?" Sera asked, clutching at my arm. "Will the magic lure us into joining?"

"You're not jumping into anything, princess," Emrys grumbled from behind us. "None of them are worthy of you."

Sera's look of concern melted away as she looked back at Emrys, letting out a nervous laugh. "That's a relief. I have enough to handle with the posse as it is."

Ahead of us, Franc threaded his way between the strategically positioned couches and beds dotting the temple floor with a singular focus, leading us to the temple's central inner sanctum. As he walked, Franc touched a shoulder here or a foot there in passing.

"What's he doing?" Sera asked me, tension knitting her brow.

"Why? Jealous?"

Sera side-eyed me, biting her lip. "Maybe? Just a little?"

I laid my hand over hers on my arm and gave her a comforting squeeze. I suppose if I didn't know this was Franc's routine, maybe I wouldn't understand it either. "I've watched him do this pattern so many times before, and I think nothing of it. As the demi-god of Dionysos, he can either rev up or curb the energy of the revelers by touch alone. He likes to moderate the festivities, just to make sure everyone's getting what they need and that things don't go off the rails."

Sera seemed to consider my words as she watched Franc. He walked up to a woman who was rolling on the ground, gently touching her head and whispering something to her. The woman's eyes cleared, and she sat up, seeming to come to her senses.

"Io! Evohe!" the woman called out in a voice that

reverberated through the temple. The revelers paused in their pursuits, a chorus of voices chanting "Io! Evohe!" in reply. Then she climbed onto the nearest couch, joining two other women as they drank from cups of wine, giggling together as they called out helpful tips to those around them.

"Turn her over. No, trust me!" said one.

"Use the feathers! Seriously, who passes on a feather bath?" asked the next.

"It's called a wheelbarrow for a reason, Luke," said the third.

The women fell back into laughter, but I didn't bother looking, choosing instead to watch Sera's reaction. From Sera's flushed cheeks and the thin sheen of sweat covering her skin, I could tell the sensual magic of this place was taking hold of her, despite her logical efforts to make sense of it all.

"I see. I mean, I really can't unsee those things." She shook her head. "No wonder Franc doesn't want people here without him. What's behind those curtains?" Sera asked me, pointing to a series of canopy enclosures running along the circular outer wall of the temple. Ivy-covered stone columns separated them with pale pink, gauzy fabric strung between them.

"Those chambers are for more private forms of entertainment," I explained. From the varied moans, grunts, and cries of pleasure issuing from all around the room, I'd guess almost all the semi-private rooms were in use.

"Nothing better than a full house worshiping at the altar," Caden declared, ever up for a party. "All hail the King of the Bacchanal!" Caden declared, his voice carrying through the room as he motioned towards Franc. A round of huzzahs echoed through the temple, ending only when Franc gave a brief bow to the crowd.

I couldn't help but laugh at the incubus, which was a welcome change of pace, considering our history together. Since we'd cleared the air and I knew he'd been working undercover and wasn't an actual drug dealer, I'd been able to let go of the anger I'd held towards Caden for far too long. It was such a welcome change to our dynamic. I was so happy to have things back to how they used to be between us when we were younger.

Franc reached the interior of the temple, which was surrounded by a reflective wall only he could open. The mirrored effect made the room feel endless, multiplying the vista of writhing bodies around us. Franc placed his hand on the wall, and a hidden lock let out a click before swinging open, motioning for us to go inside.

I moved to go in, but Sera hung back, clinging to my jacket. "What's inside?"

She was skittish as a doe fresh to the world, and I supposed I couldn't blame her. This was all unfamiliar territory, not just for Sera, but for all of us.

"It's a private, secure space where we can be alone, away from the crowd," I explained. "It'll just be us. Well, just us with a unique view."

Sera nodded as I explained, her gaze landing on each of us. Fresh ruby sparks fell from her fingertips, dancing across the skin of my arm, leaving a tingling sensation in their wake. I'd seen Sera's magic turn ghouls into torches in the Netherworld, but I didn't fear her touch or the magic that flowed through her veins, no matter how chaotic her magic behaved. She'd never hurt me or the posse, at least not intentionally, that I was certain of.

Sera nibbled at her lower lip. "I'm up for some fun, but shouldn't we be trying to solve the knot instead of playing around?"

Franc shook his head, shooting Sera a sly smile. "No, sweetheart, we need to help you burn through this overabundance of energy before we give that puzzle another go." He held out his hand in invitation.

Taneisha's warning played through my mind, and my heart gripped with worry over Sera's safety as I watched her hesitate. Sera had been helping us and protecting us from Taneisha's games for days. Now Sera needed our help, and I was determined not to fail her.

When she pulled me close, the warmth of her body like a live wire next to mine, and looked up into my eyes, I almost melted. It was like a switch had gone off within her, like she'd suddenly given over fully to the sensuous energy of the temple.

"Take me in?" she said, a pleading edge to her voice.

My panther leapt at Sera's invitation. Franc stepped aside as I scooped Sera up into my arms and strode through the doorway, leaving the others to follow us. Sera's arms threaded around my neck, her fingers running over the stubble of my hair at the nape of my neck, drawing a low growl from my throat. The frisson of her magic shot from her fingers straight down my spine to my cock, filling me with need.

Was the intensity of my reaction because of our mating bond? The magic of the temple? Or just Sera? I didn't know and right now I didn't care.

With barely a glance to get my bearings in the room, I

headed directly to the super-sized round bed in the middle of the space, illuminated only by the moon shining down through a series of skylights. A series of oak bedposts ringed the bed, each entwined with vines which grew straight up towards and across the ceiling, forming a canopy of greenery overhead. Translucent swaths of fabric hung between the bed posts covered with blooming roses, which filled the space with their heady essence. Jasmine vines grew over everything, their white blooms glowing in the moonlight and adding a touch of musk in the air.

The room was also large enough to contain a few couches, small tables, and chairs placed around the outer wall which encircled this space. From those seats, one could either watch revelers within the cella or in the outer temple through the one-way mirrored wall.

Franc did nothing halfway, especially not when it had to do with honoring his grandfather and namesake, Dionysos.

Before we reached the bed, Sera's lips were on mine, drawing almost all my available focus. I set her down on her feet, and then peeled off my jacket, hearing the leather hit the floor behind me. Sera pulled at my shirt, shredding the fabric and sending pink sparks flying as she ripped it open. I pulled off the remnants of my shirt while Sera was already unzipping my pants and sliding her hand inside.

I heard the others moving around behind me, but when I heard the door to the temple click shut, my attention was all for Sera's hand brushing against my cock. Unconcerned with the audience of my brothers, I rocked into her touch. Desperate for more than a taste, I fisted her hair in my fingers, angling her mouth to mine and claiming her with my tongue like I intended to claim the rest of her.

"I thought we were supposed to be burning off Sera's energy, not the other way around?" Em asked.

My panther bristled at the possessive edge in the demigod's tone, but I forgot about it a moment later when Sera freed my erection from my pants.

I heard Caden chuckle as he strolled around the room. "A little of column A, a little of column B. What's the harm?" He sighed. "I love a good show."

Em grumbled something, but I was kicking off my shoes and shucking off my pants like my life depending on it. Sera's hands never left my skin. Was she as hungry for my touch as I was for hers? My panther purred appreciatively at the contact, soaking in her affection.

Kissing her with a singular focus, I backed us towards the bed, finding and unzipping the back of her dress along the way. I let out a whine of frustration as I wrested her arms away from me so I could slip off the dress' barely there straps. As soon as I freed her from them, Sera's hands found my chest, leaving a trail of nearly electric sparks in their wake across my skin. I hissed; an edge of pain bound up with the pleasure of her touch. I tried to be careful sliding the slip of her dress down and around her hips, yet I felt something give as I worked the fabric over the curve of her hips.

It felt natural to sink down to my knees before our mate, bringing my face square to what must have been the most useless underwear ever invented.

I ran my fingers across the silky fabric studded with glittering gemstones, rewarded with a shiver rolling across

Sera's flesh. "These are gorgeous, but I can see right through them."

"Leave it to Taneisha to dress me ridiculously," Sera replied.

"Oh, I disagree," Franc said. "The Fae might be unstable, but her fashion choices are immaculate. I'd offer to help, but your claws will shred that silk soon enough."

The image Franc planted in my head was just too good to pass up, and he knew it. I allowed my panther to surge to the surface, and my fingernails sharpened into pointed tips. I slid the sharp edges between Sera's velvety skin and the silk, eliciting a gasp from her lips.

"Too much?" I asked, watching her expression for any sign of fear.

A hint of a smile curled her lips. "I trust you, Marcos. Bring it on, kitty cat."

My inner beast purred at her nickname. My claws ripped through the flimsy fabric like butter, and I brought the underwear to my nose, breathing in Sera's feminine musk. I heard the growl escape my throat before I even realized I was doing it, and my animal instincts took over.

Mindful of my claws, I carefully gripped Sera's hips, urging her down onto the bed as I laid a line of kisses along her stomach. I moved between her thighs, running my tongue along her skin, hungry for a taste of her. When my mouth found her center, I couldn't help but smile at her low moan of pleasure. I went to work with my tongue while I massaged my hands along her inner thighs, lightly pressing my claws against her flesh. By the way she ground and bucked against me, I knew the thrill was a welcome addition.

"More, Marcos!" she demanded.

I redoubled my efforts, circling my tongue around her clit in a way that caused her to buck against me with every flick.

I felt movement on the bed next to us as Liam and Emrys joined in. Sera writhed as a shirtless Liam sucked and played with her nipples, while Emrys took her hands, pinning them down above her head.

Emrys' eyes were only for Sera, his expression one of raw hunger. I recognized the emotion in him because I felt the same way towards Sera, deep within my soul. Gratefully, Emrys didn't appear affected by her magical outburst, and I was glad he'd stepped up to help shield the rest of us. I didn't believe Sera would intend to hurt us, her mates, with her magic, but I agreed with his cautious step.

A cascade of violet sparks flew from her hands and around Emrys as she came apart beneath my and Liam's attentions, her cries of passion captured by Liam's mouth. I growled in triumph, feeling her body shiver against my mouth.

I could have moved aside for one of my brothers, but I wasn't done with her yet. We were here to wear Sera out, and I wouldn't step down from the challenge. Liam left the bed, and my attention shifted entirely to Sera. I kissed my way up her abdomen, flicking my tongue across her nipple as I centered my hips between her thighs and pressed my erection against her swollen core. I slid myself against her, teasing out the moment, as I waited for Sera to open her eyes and meet my gaze.

"What are you waiting for?" Sera asked. Despite being pinned down on the bed by Emrys' and myself, Sera was in charge in this situation, and I had no illusions that she was the one calling the shots.

"Just that, my mate," I murmured, before pressing my length into her. I fell onto her then, pumping with a slow, steady pace I knew would drive her crazy. Sera wrapped her legs around me, driving the heels of her shoes into my lower back, urging me to speed up. In return, I ran my claws across her skin, guessing from her earlier reaction that the combination of sharp sensation and the edge of risk would drive her passion higher.

Not that I'd ever cut her, but the way her eyes dilated as she watched my claws dance along her skin, confirming my suspicions that she liked a bit of risk along with her pleasure. I lost myself in the moment, moving within her, feeling Sera give herself over to me.

As she neared yet another peak, my panther itched to claim her, to make her ours. Yet I knew this wasn't the time.

Waves of power rolled off of Sera, and for a moment I could swear her skin glittered with energy. Everywhere we touched, a near electric sensation passed between us, the sharp intensity stealing my breath away. When I caught my breath, my release followed soon after with shuddering intensity. By the time I recovered and pulled myself off her, Sera's skin was once again normal.

Sera pulled her hands from Emrys' grip and turned over onto her hands and knees before sinking sensuously back onto her hips. She reminded me of a sphinx, her long, raven hair falling around her head and shoulders like a lion.

"Liam," she demanded, crooking a finger his way. "Come back here."

MAGE IN THE STREETS

LIAM

I glanced around at the others, seeing four other sets of eyes all intensely watching our mate from around the room. Emrys still sat on the bed, his expression uncharacteristically sober. Marcos had pulled his pants back on and was pouring himself a glass of water while still keeping his focus on Sera. Franc and Caden lounged on a sofa across the room, Caden absentmindedly stroking Franc's cock while their focus was otherwise on Sera.

"Liam," Sera sing-songed my name this time, bringing my attention back to her. I was powerless to resist her call.

I hesitated only a moment before peeling off my pants and joining Sera on the bed. I had thought after the two very thorough orgasms Marcos had wrung from her, she'd have been more worn out, but from the heady need in her gaze, Sera was only getting started.

"I could never refuse your call, mate," I replied. "What do you have in mind?"

Sera subvocalized a growl in reply, causing blood to flood even faster to my already growing erection.

As I drew near, she rose onto her knees, the brilliant moonlight filtering in from the skylights above, painting her features with stark angles. Sera's hands skimmed the hard planes of my chest. Then she wrapped her arms around me, pulling me close. I couldn't help myself. Hungry to taste her, I brought her lips up to mine, thrusting my tongue deep into the heat of her mouth.

My wolf's urge to claim Sera had become the ever-present backbeat to all of my thoughts, but in this moment my beast relented, at peace under the comfort of her touch.

"I want you," she growled, her eyes lit with inner fire. If I hadn't known better, I'd have thought she was a shifter too.

"Then take me," I baited her.

Sera shifted her weight on the bed, pushing me backwards. I let myself fall, and she pounced upon me, straddling my hips and pushing me inside her in one smooth motion. I gasped out, the pleasure of being suddenly sheathed deep within her silken warmth almost too much for me to handle. I took hold of her thighs, pinning her in place while I worked to rein myself in.

By the wicked smile on her face, Sera knew she had me right on the edge. She planted a firm hand on my chest, and I grabbed it by the wrist, my wolf begging me to take control. To roll her underneath me. To take charge and show her everything I had to give. To claim her as mine.

But that wasn't what Sera needed from me right now, so I relented, allowing her to call the shots. She held me in place as she gyrated her hips in at first slight, but ever-widening circles, against me. I bucked up into her, quickly finding a rhythm that served us both. Crackles of power cascaded through her hair, their pale glow illuminating the surrounding space. She leaned down over me, and I cupped her breasts in my hands, rolling her hard nipples between my fingers. I glimpsed what looked like lightning flash through her chestnut brown eyes, but it was gone a moment later. Sera appeared unaffected, lost to our passions.

When our inevitable peak arrived, Sera threw back her head and cried out as she came apart around me. A wave of sparks flew from her hands, covering my chest with an abrupt fire that burned for mere milliseconds before scattering around the room. Her power rolled over me and through me, the sensation so intense I swore she branded herself into my very cells. I followed Sera into the abyss a moment later, the edge of pain bringing my pleasure into sharp focus.

I worried for her, but when Sera cast her gaze my way again, her luscious smile set me at ease. I swore I heard a round of cheers circle around through the revelers in the temple, but for the life of me, I couldn't be bothered to find out what they were going on about this time.

"Are you all right?" I asked, trailing my fingers across her stomach.

She nodded. "I am. I feel amazing. Like I could float right out of here."

I grinned but worry fretted at the back of my mind. If she was still this energized, then we had a way to go to burn through the wild magic coursing through Sera's veins.

Emrys moved closer until he pressed up against Sera's thigh. He ran a hand through her hair to tame her wild tresses. Magic crackled against his fingers, but he gave no sign of the electric fire bothering him.

"Are you feeling any relief, darling?" Emrys asked, cupping her cheek.

She leaned into his touch like the hopeful thirsty at an empty well. The smile Sera shone his way had a hungry edge to it, almost frenzied, and I knew we still had a long way to go to help her. It was then I realized how much she needed each of us. No wonder fate had matched her with all five of us.

"I crave you, Em," she replied, before running a hand across my chest, gripping at my flesh. "All of you."

MAENAD IN THE SHEETS

EMRYS

When I scooped Sera up, pulling her from off Liam, he didn't object. The shifter looked unusually worn out from their encounter, so I didn't doubt he'd welcome me stepping in. Sera settled into my lap, entwining sweaty limbs around my body, kissing my cheeks and then down my throat, nibbling as she went.

If I had my way, I'd carry her out of this club, take her to my loft downtown, and have my way with her for days on end. But there was no leaving, at least not until we'd unraveled the fae's knot.

"Hmm," she purred against my skin. "You always smell so good." She sighed. "Cedar and sage. Like the desert itself."

Considering my Isis-born lineage, I should smell of the desert. I looked down at the wild creature in my arms and gently stroked her back. Sera's skin had an almost radiant quality, but perhaps it was just an effect of the bright moonlight?

I felt the smile tugging at my lips, despite my concern for Sera. "I suppose that's fitting."

Our affections were bringing about a change in her, yet doubt gnawed at my gut. Was it enough to burn off the magic running wild within her? "Does it feel like the magic is dissipating?"

Sera nestled closer to me, rocking against my building erection, but her eyes were lost in reflection. "Some of the magic released, but the rest is shifting somehow." She looked up at me, anxiety knitting her brow. "It still feels like too much, but I think I can manage better now."

I'd taken the brunt of her energetic blast when she was with Marcos, with no problems. Having resurrection and accelerated healing in my back pocket wasn't the most active of powers for a demi-god, but they'd never failed me. I'd figured my physical resilience would withstand anything Sera had to dish out, and so far, I hadn't been wrong.

I tucked Sera's hair behind her ear. Charged sparks fell from her tresses like tiny stars, dancing for moments upon the silky sheets beneath us. "Ready for another round?"

She sucked on her lower lip, rolling it between her teeth before answering. "I need you, Em."

I clutched her tight against me, her demand bringing out a visceral response. I wanted to hold on to Sera and never let go. She'd brought me back from the darkness in the maze. I'd do whatever it took to free her from the cursed knot's power.

"You have me, Sera," I whispered. "Spirit and soul."

I laid Sera back on the bed, shifting my weight over her, and her body opened beneath me. Her pliant, soft body was at odds with the strong-willed, determined, and fierce spirit I knew her to be. Her trust humbled me. Although I couldn't wait to bury myself in her and hear Sera screaming my name, I had to see what my abilities might aid the process.

I placed my hand over her heart and stilled, open to what my mind's eye might reveal. Potent lines of power ran through her body from head to toe, radiating outwards from her heart with such intensity as I'd never witnessed before. Even knowing the power of Sera's magic, I hadn't quite expected to find this reservoir of power lurking within her. However, flowing through her body ran a shadowy magic which twisted and knotted like bindweed around those radiating conduits.

My eyes flashed open to find Sera staring right back at me.

"That bad?" She asked, worry creasing the skin around her eyes.

"I've seen worse," I responded, my flippant tone sounding hollow to my own ears. "I'm sure I can heal you, though. Will you let me try?"

Sera's hand came up and cupped my cheek. "Do your worst," she said, but there was humor in her gaze.

I shed my clothes faster than I thought possible, my focus fully on Sera. I moved over her, laying my body gently over hers, aiming for the most skin contact possible. My erection pressed against her inner thigh, but my immediate goal wasn't to claim her, but to heal her. The heat from her body nearly scorched my skin, but it did not deter me. She needed me now more than ever, and I would be here for Sera, whatever she needed.

I focused my thoughts, accessing my reservoir of magic. I felt the breath of life rush through me, eager to burst forth. When I exhaled, a shimmer formed in the air around my breath. A look of wonder passed over Sera's face as my breath came into contact with her skin. Everywhere it touched, she glowed.

"More," she demanded, writhing beneath me.

I captured her lips with my own and breathed out, filling her with the breath of life. The heady sensation of our magic combining and melding together forced all the thoughts from my mind. I was lost in Sera. In the touch of her soul against mine. The effervescent glow of her skin. The hypersensitivity of every nerve as we undulated against the bed together.

I needed her like I needed breath. I never wanted to let this treasure of a woman go.

"Inside me. Now," Sera gasped out between kisses.

I was happy to oblige. Combined as our magics were in this moment, the heightened sensation of entering Sera nearly overwhelmed me, and I had to take a moment to adjust and savor the divine feel of her surrounding me. Heat poured off the both of us, sweat slicking our skin. Her limbs wound around me, locking me against her.

Beyond the pleasure, I barely kept my focus around on the flow of Sera's magic. Even as my magic worked to free hers of the fae's shadowy binding, I felt resistance at every turn. As the pressure built between our bodies, so it also built between our magics.

Sera's release came like a shock wave over both of us, with mine following along not long thereafter. Energy rippled out from us on the bed in the middle of the room. I heard vases crash to the floor and chairs knock over. Even the walls surrounding the cella rang like they'd been hit like a gong.

But none of that was of consequence to me. I focused on Sera's energy, relieved to find the fae's energetic constraints no longer wound through her body. Spent in every way, I collapsed against her, the sound of our panting echoing in the now silent chamber.

"It's gone, Em. You did it."

Sera squirmed to move, and it took me more effort than it should have to roll myself off of her. I laid there for a minute, just breathing and staring up at the moon through the skylights.

But while I was exhausted, Sera seemed somehow re-energized. She sat up on the bed, stretching her arms overhead before shaking out her raven hair. Sera leaned down over me, planting a delicate kiss on my forehead.

"I swear you almost shot me into the stars. Are you okay?"

Sera wasn't wrong. My power reserves had been drained by helping her. Yet, seeing her unabashed smile, my heart sang. "Not to worry, my love. I'll rebound soon. Besides, I'd do it all again to see your radiant smile."

CIRCLE ROUND HIM THRICE

SERA

"You delivered a lot more than a smile," I replied, unable to wipe the grin off my face. My body practically hummed with energy, the hair at the back of my neck soaked with sweat as heat poured off me.

"You know you can count on me," Em whispered, his gaze only for me. He looked so exhausted, with shadows darkening under his eyes, I would have worried about him, except I knew with his healing and resurrection powers that he was nearly indestructible.

An ethereal, wind-like melody carried from somewhere in the outer temple, tugging at my curiosity, calling me to investigate. Through the one-way mirror I saw revelers milling about, an impassioned, wide-eyed smile catching my attention.

Liam and Marcos had regained their pants and appeared to be focused on the revelers. I could see them whispering but couldn't make out what they were saying.

Franc, who'd been lounging with Caden on a sofa watching us, stood up and walked over, his gaze assessing me. He held his cock in his hand, stroking it leisurely. He watched me like he was weighing me, and a thrill ran through me. What did the demi-god have in mind next?

Caden, who was still somehow fully dressed, followed Franc over to the bed. I ran a hand down Em's chest, lightly scratching him with my nails, and he arched into my touch. There was a frenetic edge to the energy in the temple, and to my guys, that had me eager for what might happen next.

"Looks like the party's still raging out there," I said, attempting to break the tension.

Franc arched a brow. "The party never stops in the temple, and it's not over for you either, little rabbit."

With a little shaky effort, Emrys pushed himself up. "I healed Sera from the lock the fae's magic geas had on her powers. She's free of it now. You don't need to keep pushing her to wear her out."

"Oh, I may not have to, yet I really want to," Franc growled. "Are you ready to admit how much you need us? To accept that we're yours, and you're ours?"

Was he really going to push this again? Now? I threw back my head, my laugh ringing off the walls. When I took a deep breath and looked around, all five of them were staring at me, taking Franc's question more seriously than I did.

Something about their communal attitude just revved up my need to dig in my heels. "How about we worry about this later, when we're not stuck on a series of side quests for a delusional fae? Or worried someone might die? Or lose Franc's mask to Taneisha's destructive whims?"

"These aren't trivial side quests," Emrys snapped back. "This is our future Franc's asking about."

"Everything's a side quest," I said, rolling my eyes.

Caden crossed his arms and huffed out a deep sigh. "You're making light of how we've bonded together, so you don't have to face your fears over an uncertain and uncharted future. Your life was predictable and easy before fate stamped you with those mate markings. To add insult to injury, you hunger for each of us, yet only grudgingly admit it." The Caden had the gall to smile, showing off that adorable dimple of his. "Did I leave anything out?"

My jaw dropped, and I could no longer meet his gaze. Leave it to the incubus to go right for my jugular, and damn him, but I couldn't deny it. I held my tongue, afraid of what might come out.

"Oh, this feels like the perfect time," Franc walked up to the edge of the bed. "You're going to figure out how much you need us. Want us." Franc reached for the gauzy fabric hanging between the bedposts and tore off a strip. The sound of rending fabric did something funny to my thoughts, and when Franc held the pink fabric out in front of him in invitation, my insides clenched.

"What's that supposed to be?" I asked, hearing the building anxiety in my voice.

"Your blindfold. May I?" Franc answered, the dare plain in his eyes.

Not yet deciding, I crawled over to him, touching the silky fabric. "Why?"

"Em's healing may have freed you from the geas, but you'd still over thinking. This is an invitation to let go."

I bit my lower lip. "Losing control is not exactly safe for anyone around me."

Franc tucked my hair behind my ear, his "We're your mates. Trust that we can handle whatever you can dish out. Trust us to take you to the edge, over the edge, and into the space beyond."

I recalled the time I'd torched a bunch of ghouls with my mage fire, but I knew that wasn't what Franc meant. Something deep within in me craved what he was offering, although I couldn't quite name the reason. That, for once, I didn't have to be in control, was strangely seductive. Knowing Franc would be the one driving me over the edge quenched a thirst I didn't know I had.

"Okay," I nodded, and Franc tied the blindfold around my head, blocking out the moonlight and casting me into darkness.

The next moment, Franc's lips were on mine as he pulled me into a rough, hungry embrace. His tongue sought mine with desperate hunger, wiping my mind clear of my inner turmoil. He urged me to back up on the bed, joining me there. Pressed against him with his erection twitching against my stomach, my need to have him almost overwhelmed me.

I could blame the sensuous magic of this place, but it didn't create these urges and wants in me. The magic of Velvet and the temple only lowered the threshold to my inhibitions, paving the way for me to take what I wanted without second-guessing myself.

Taking the lead, I kissed my way down Franc's stomach to his cock, pulling his girth between my lips so I could taste the salty tang of him. The bed dipped behind me, and I gasped as a tongue zeroed in on my clit. Not knowing for sure which of my guys was toying with me short circuited something in my brain. I tried to focus on managing Franc, but I kept losing the pace to my pleasure.

I jumped as someone slapped my ass, but it couldn't have been Franc, as his hands were fisting my hair.

Franc groaned. "I think our mage needs some help with her focus."

"Let me try something," Caden replied from between my thighs. Again, I felt the bed move as he readjusted, and a moment later, he pressed into me from behind.

I slid Franc out of my mouth, groaning at Caden's sudden entry. The feel of his cock, with the ball bearings he'd had implanted under his skin of his shaft, was unique and intense.

"That's not helping, Caden," I swore.

He pulled my hips back onto his cock, giving me the full length of him. "You want me to stop?"

"No," I breathed out, half gasping, half groaning.

"Good. Now, I've got an idea for that focus problem of yours. Give me your hands." Caden's hands slid down my arms, caressing as he moved. He took one hand, pulling it back behind me, and then the other, gripping both wrists firmly. "Lean forward, sweetheart."

I hesitated, unsure what he was doing. Plus, I didn't want to fall on my face.

"Trust me," he whispered in my ear.

My heart skipped a beat. Of course, I trusted Caden. I trusted all of them. Although I couldn't see, I knew they wouldn't do anything that would hurt me. The tension melted out of me, and I leaned forward. Caden's grip on me didn't falter, and soon I felt the tip of Franc's erection brush against my lips.

"Oh," I exclaimed, finally catching on. I flicked out my tongue around Franc's cock, encouraging them both.

Caden set our pace, grinding into me as he controlled the depth and speed of the head I was giving Franc. Franc's hands gripped my hair, encouraging my movements. Before long, the intensity of the combined giving and taking pushed me over the edge to my release, and I writhed in their arms, helpless against the orgasm rolling over me. Another wave of power shot through me, and again the cella walls rang like a gong, reverberating from the impact with my magic. Franc and Caden both grunted, but they rode out the moment, wringing the pleasure from my body.

When Franc peaked soon after, Caden backed me off the demi-god's cock and let go of my arms, pinning my hips back against him as he cried out in what I assumed was his native demonic tongue as he exploded into me.

"That was amazing," I uttered.

Caden chuckled. "If you like that, I've got other tricks you might like, too."

I caught my breath, expecting my blindfold to come off, but someone scooped me up, flipped me over onto my back, and covered me with their masculine heat. I thought it was Liam over me, but I didn't have time to be sure before others joined him. Hands massaged my breasts, rolling the hard points of my nipples between adept fingertips. A mouth covered my pussy as fingers stroked inside of me. Hands massaged and teased my skin, making every inch of me come alive.

I recognized Franc's lips on my own, his taste sweet as a port and rich as a cabernet. My head swam in the clouds. I didn't know who was where, doing what, but I knew I didn't want them to stop. I recalled Franc's promise to push me beyond, and I felt like I could see the threshold from here. I felt like I could, and would, burst at the seams at any moment. Every sensitive part of my body was being teased at once, and it didn't take them long to wring the first orgasm out of me. Then the second. Then another, and another, leaving me rasping for breath. Each peak drew wave after wave of energy from me, pouring out as if from my very spirit.

Instead of tiring me, each wave built on the last, lifting me higher. I opened my internal floodgates, allowing the energy to burn through and out of me. The emotions and needs of my lovers flooded through my mind. Their drive to mate with me. Their hunger for my love. Their strength to protect and shelter me. Their need for my acceptance.

"It's too much," I panted. "I'm losing control."

Franc's touch was gentle on my face. "Good. Sometimes a touch of madness is the path to breakthroughs, and sometimes you have to let the magic run wild in order to reach a new level of control."

His reassurance calmed my fears, and I let go. Completely.

My next release didn't feel like any orgasm I'd ever had before. It was as if lightning had shot through me, leaving nothing but raw power in its wake. It obliterated all conscious thought, and I lost all sensation in my body, so much so that I wondered if I still had a body at all.

My ears rang as the glass walls surrounding the cella shattered and fell like rain to the floor, opening our previous secluded space to the outer temple. The touches of my lovers finally ceased. I ripped off my blindfold and pushed myself upright, the sound of my heart beating like a drum in my chest. Standing revelers filled the outer temple, no longer lost to their own pleasures, but with their eyes turned to me. Waiting. The murmur of a chant arose from the throng. I couldn't quite make out the words, but I felt it in my bones.

On the bed, my guys lay strewn in a circle around me, unconscious. Anxiety flooded me. What had I done? But when I touched them, they were warm and breathing. Franc even moved and groaned like he was trying to say something but couldn't quite rouse himself.

Unlike them, the spark of life surged within me. I heard far-off drums calling to me, echoing the pulsing beat thrumming in my chest. The rhythm of the reveler's chants matched the faint but insistent drumbeat.

I had to go. I had to answer the call.

Now!

I jumped up and clambered over my men, ripping down a swath of pink silk from between the canopy posts. After I wrapped it around myself, I snatched my makeshift blindfold from the middle of the bed and tied it around my waist. I stepped down off the bed, took hold of the post, and pulled it free. I pounded it on the ground, hearing the earth reverberate beneath my feet. Pink silk trailed out behind me like a sail as I stormed into the awaiting crowd, which parted before my upheld staff.

CLOSE YOUR EYES WITH HOLY DREAD

FRANC

I wrestled against the fatigue which weighed heavy on my limbs, dragging myself up just in time to see the last of the revelers pouring out of the far end of my wrecked temple. The mirror wall separating the cella from the main temple area had shattered outward. Couches had been overturned. Togas laid cast off in pools of spilled wine.

The lights might be dim, but I could feel the disturbing, but unmistakable buzz of the sanguine trail of blood the revelers had left in their wake.

I'd seen some crazy nights in the temple, but the blood? That was new.

The call of the drum pounded against the inside of my mind. I took a deep breath and pushed the summons to the back of my mind. I couldn't silence the beat, but I wouldn't do my brothers or Sera any good if I lost myself to the seductive thrall.

"What the hell happened?" Liam demanded, groaning as he rolled to his side. He had a wary look in his gaze as he took in the remains of the temple, which I imagined was only slightly better than whatever grim expression painted my face right about now.

We were all arranged haphazardly around the cella's massive bed, placed wherever we'd fallen when Sera's power had erupted. All of us were naked, and I wasn't sure everyone was even conscious.

"I'm not entirely sure. Roll call. Is anyone injured?" I asked.

"I feel bruised all over, but I think nothing's broken. Group sex with you all could have killed me," Caden groaned. The only part moving on him was his mouth. "What did we do wrong? Was it too much all at once? Too fast? Too many O's?"

"That's a hell of a confession for an incubus," Marcos replied, pulling himself up off the floor. He glanced around, took in the carnage, and then hunted for his clothes. "Too much sex? I'll mark this day on my calendar, and we can celebrate it with an orgy of abstinence annually."

Caden laughed and then grabbed at his sides. "Oh, fuck you, Marcos! I'll banish you to the Netherworld if you tell anyone."

Marcos smiled, but his voice came out with a low grumble. "Little late for that threat. Been there, done that."

I shook my head. Finally pulling myself to my feet, I searched for my own clothes, only finding my slacks, socks, and shoes. "You're full of bluster for someone who isn't even moving, Caden."

"I'm getting to it!" He tried to roll over, and then let out a whine. "Ow! Why does everything hurt so much?"

I'd point out how melodramatic he was being, but what

would be the point? Caden would likely take my badgering and run with it.

"Em," I barked at him. He laid face down with his head off the edge of the bed, his golden skin twitching visibly across his shoulders at the sound of my voice. I hadn't been worried for him because of his regeneration abilities, yet I relaxed just a little to see him moving again.

The bedding muffled Emrys' reply. "I'm going after Sera."

I patted his leg. "You're not going anywhere until you recover, golden boy."

"I'm going," he mumbled.

"We're going after her. Together," I replied.

Em muttered something against the silk sheets. Whatever, I'd worry about him when he pulled himself together.

"I'm gonna ask again," Liam, now on his feet, pulled on pants I was pretty sure were his. "What happened, Franc?"

"I'm not sure. I need a minute to process."

"Yeah? Cause I don't," Liam snapped back, pulling on his shirt. His green eyes cut into me like a blade. "You brought us all here to help Sera burn off her excess energy, to free her from the fae's geas. You encouraged her to let loose and embrace a little madness." Liam swept his hand around at the mess. "This wasn't just a little madness, Franc. Look around. This was a lot."

I ran a hand through my sweat-dampened curly hair. "It went further than I intended."

"So, then you didn't mean for her to go full maenad?" Caden asked, looking at me with just one eye open. "Just semi-maenad?"

I sighed. "Of course, I didn't."

Caden shook his head. "Everyone knows you never go full maenad," he muttered.

I rolled my eyes at the demon's poorly timed humor. Next thing I knew, a growl erupted from Liam as he launched himself at me. Marcos intercepted him at the last minute, taking the brunt of the hit the wolf had intended for me.

"Slow it down, brother," Marcos said to Liam. "We're all on the same side here."

I met Liam's gaze without flinching, but grateful for Marcos' always level head. Liam's anger simmered for a few moments, and I wondered if I'd soon be fighting his wolf, but he remained in control.

"This is not a joke," Liam spat out. "Sera is gone. She needed us, and you just pushed her over the edge."

I saw Caden and Em moving out of the corners of my vision as they roused and dressed, but I kept my focus on Liam. "You're right, that didn't go like I'd planned. I underestimated the impact of the fae's magic on Velvet and the people inside."

My admission kicked the fire right out of Liam, revealing the anxiety driving his emotions. He gave a single nod and backed up a step. It felt like we all shared a collective sigh.

"What's next? How do we get her back from the revelers?" Liam asked.

"We don't, at least not yet," I explained. Marcos turned to me, and then I had multiple glowering supes to contend with as they all turned disbelieving and confused faces toward me. I needed to save Sera, Velvet, and my brothers, and to do that, I needed their help. "Hear me out?"

"Go on," Marcos said.

"Sera's freed of the geas and is now running through the proverbial hills of madness. Thus, the knot's magic is no longer entwined with hers, so she's safe from it. This gives me an opportunity to solve that puzzle."

"Are you seriously putting your mask, and your club, before Sera's safety?" Liam asked, his eyes lit with banked fire.

"No. Quite the opposite. If we run off after Sera and the revelers in the state they're in now, we risk being caught up in the throes of madness right along with them. However, if we can free my legacy from the fae's knot, I can retake control of the magic, Velvet, and the revelers. It's a strategic move. Free Velvet and protect Sera at the same time."

"You can do what you want, but I'm going after Sera," Em said. "I'm not leaving her to the whims of your revelers."

"I'm going with you," Liam added, to which Em grudgingly nodded.

"We need to stick together," I pressed. "We're stronger together." Em and Liam didn't argue, but I could tell I hadn't swayed them. "I assure you; Sera is safe from the fae and the revelers."

"You're so certain of that?" Em asked me.

I hesitated only a moment, my gaze flicking to the blood trail the revelers had left. It was enough that Em noticed and arched a brow my way. "She's powerful," I continued. "More than any of us even realized. Tonight, Sera tapped into something within herself that she didn't have access to before."

"All the more reason she needs us," Liam said.

Liam's puppy dog inclinations were really grating on my nerves, but I couldn't say that out loud. "We need to trust Sera to follow her process. Besides, if she were here, she'd tell us to never split the party."

"Split the party?" Marcos asked.

"It's a gaming term she used once," I explained.

"Cool story, bro," Em replied, shutting down the conversation. "But with Sera gone, the party's already split. Ready?" he asked Liam.

Liam looked at me and Marcos and then nodded to Em. "Right behind you."

Em and Liam walked off without a backwards glance. Were they right? Should we all head after Sera first?

No. I trusted that Sera, empowered with maenad energy, could manage the revelers just fine. I needed to unravel the fae's knot. That was the path toward freeing all of us trapped within Velvet's walls.

I hated to see us split up, but I knew better than to fight Liam and Em, even worrying about what might happen. So far, when we had separated during the fae's quests, things had only gotten worse for us. At least Marcos and Caden stayed behind, which struck a chord of relief within me.

"Back to the dance floor?" Marcos prodded, as if sensing my hesitation.

I nodded. "Let's give that knot another try."

Caden clapped me on the back. "They'll be fine. Lead on."

We exited the now quiet temple, finding only small groups of patrons milling through the gardens outside. I steered us around the raucous laughter and loud voices, not wanting to get sidelined. When we reached the archway to the dance floor, the music was still booming, and the room was again filled with swaying, gyrating bodies. Any other night I might have taken comfort in the familiar sultry, sweaty mojo, but knowing everyone here was trapped shattered the illusion.

Marcos led the way through the crowd with Caden and I following in his brawny wake. I heard more than one dancer growl and groan as we passed through them, and I couldn't help but feel like things were even more on edge than when we'd left. Just how long could my patrons hold out after days of partying? Even more reason to solve the fae's knot puzzle as soon as possible.

We reached the center of the dance floor and found my mask remained. Still surrounded by the fae's magical knot, it glowed like liquid pink neon flowing around it. The dancers gave the area a wide berth, giving us plenty of room to work without feeling crowded.

Fear gripped my heart as Taneisha emerged from the crowd, her face filled with tension. "What's the plan this time, perkadelics?"

"Less mage, more me," I replied, hoping my bravado would translate into confidence. "What brings you here?"

She shrugged. "I sensed you guys disentangled Sera's energy from my knot, so I figured you'd show up here next." She looked around, frowning. "I think you lost someone? Someones?" The question hung in the air.

"Yeah, we split the party," Caden replied.

"That doesn't seem wise, considering your history," Taneisha said.

I held up my hand, stalling their conversation. "Are you here to help or heckle, T?"

Taneisha pursed her lips. "Both, definitely both."

"You're here to help? How? And why now?" I demanded.

"I'd figured you might have questions? Need a little direction?"

Whatever this new game was, I didn't want any of it from the fae.

"You want to help? How about you detangle the magic yourself?" I asked.

"Eh, afraid I can't do that, champ. Only you can solve this puzzle." Taneisha smiled, but when we didn't smile back, her expression soured. "And, no pressure, but you, and your revelers, are running out of time. If you don't diffuse this time bomb quickly, things are gonna start spiraling out of control."

Like I couldn't figure that out on my own? I certainly didn't need the added confirmation pressing down on me. I had to settle my nerves and get this knot solved.

"Just back off and give me space to focus," I said.

Caden leaned close, his hand brushing across my back. "You've got this." We shared a look, one where I was pretty sure he was more confident than I, and then he took a step back.

I stood before the glowing box of woven magic, trying to decide on a tactic. Taneisha had said only I could solve this puzzle. I knew the fae couldn't lie outright, so I trusted in those words. I reached out and tentatively touched the vines, relieved when the magic didn't burn. Instead of the electric heat I'd expected after seeing Sera thrown across the room after touching the same box, my fingers met with a cool chill. To my surprise, I could manipulate the threads, pulling and testing them.

I spent a few minutes working at the box, fascinated as

the magical vines behaved like they were practically alive. Just as I'd freed one tendril, the tip would seek another and coil back up like bindweed. I'd created an opening, although it wasn't yet big enough to pull out the mask. I knew with enough time I'd get there.

Caden's leg brushed up against me, and I cursed at the distraction. "Uh, Franc?" Caden stammered. "The natives are getting restless."

I couldn't tear my eyes away from the puzzle before me. "I need more time."

A scream rang through the room and the tinge of something feral laced with fear shot through the air. I tried to maintain focus, but suddenly I was losing the battle against the magical vines. I felt the energy in the room like another limb, and for the first time, there were tones and shades to the vibrations I didn't recognize.

"Damn it," I whispered. Was it the fae's magic? Sera's? Both? This was my home. My sacred space. How could everything feel so foreign?

"I see blood," Caden said. "What the hell are they doing?"

"They're biting each other," Marcos added, his voice tense.

"Just a few more minutes!" I called out.

"Is that an arm?" Taneisha let out a nervous giggle. "Ew, who starts with the fingers? That's just unsanitary."

Marcos cleared his throat in what I'd come to dub as his 'time to quit your bullshit' intro, his hand coming to rest on my shoulder. "We need to get out of here, clear the room, and then try again later."

I almost had it...

"We're out of time!" Caden yelled.

As Marcos lifted me to my feet and dragged me across the dance floor, I finally looked up. Caden pulled Taneisha along beside us as blood smeared faces in the crowd watched us retreat.

And then the blooded followed us.

HE ON HONEY-DEW HATH FED

FRANC

"I've seen some weird shit across multiple realms, but what the fuck is wrong with them?" Caden hollered.

We ran out into the gardens, which were deserted again, ducked into a deserted alcove, and then paused to catch our breath.

"Which way?" Taneisha asked, pulling herself away from Caden.

"Why are you even here with us?" I demanded. I wasn't sure why her presence unnerved me so, but the last thing I wanted was the fae hanging around and finding more things to vex us with.

"I swore to Sera that I wouldn't let any of you die. From the looks of things, you need all the help you can get."

I got up in her face, but she didn't even flinch. "If you'd wanted to help, why not just release my legacy from your magical trap and let everyone in the club go?"

The fae smirked back at me. "I'm not relenting an inch

more than I must, demi-god. Your inability to work out the puzzle is your own undoing, and I'm relishing every moment. If you 'almost die' yourselves, that's not on me!"

People slowly began to emerge from the dance hall into the gardens, sniffing at the air and howling at the moon.

"Shh, table it, kids," Marcos whispered, interrupting us. "Unless you have a better plan, I think we should catch up with the others. We'll need everyone to help us clear the dance hall and give you enough time to unravel that knot."

I took a deep breath, centering myself. Marcos was right. I couldn't play the fool to the fae's games, and if she wouldn't leave, then we'd just have to tolerate her.

"You did a circuit earlier of the club and its recent modifications," I said to Marcos, my voice low. "Any idea where the revelers might have headed?"

He wobbled his head from side to side. "The direction they left the temple earlier might have led to the new pool room. I'd advise we head that way and watch for signs of their passing. Such a large group shouldn't be too hard to locate."

Caden grabbed Marcos and me by the arms, pulling us in close. "Let me get this straight. We're headed toward a pack of wild revelers, followed by maniac cannibal dancers, with a mentally unstable and vindictive fae as our sidekick?"

My stomach clenched as Marcos and I stared at Caden for a moment, and then we all three turned to look at Taneisha, who we knew had heard every word.

Her eyes shone in the moonlight as the sweetest of smiles crept across her face. "First, you don't know for sure that all the dancers are cannibals. That's unfair labeling them all like that. Second, I appreciate being included as your sidekick." She leaned close and patted Caden on the cheek, and I swore I could feel the whoosh of wind as his balls retreated, but at least this time he held his tongue. "This is a positive evolution in our group dynamic. Don't you think so?"

"Definitionally, a kidnapper can't really be on the same team as their captives," I said.

Taneisha sighed. "You'll come around." There were more hoots and hollers as more people came out into the garden. "Are we waiting for the maybe-cannibals to catch up, or what?"

Marcos motioned with his head. "Follow me and stay in the shadows. There's a hidden passage behind that tree."

We crept along in a line with Marcos taking up the lead, Taneisha and Caden behind him, and then me following up the rear so I could keep an eye on the fae. Marcos moved through the shadows with a panther shifter's grace. We rounded the tree and met with a wall of ivy. Marcos deftly pulled aside the vines, directing us into what looked like the mouth of a cave.

"Since when do I have a cave?" I muttered.

"Oh, don't you just love it?" Taneisha crowed back at me.

A screech erupted in the gardens, saving me from having to reply. Marcos and I moved back around the tree, looking around the gardens for the source. Marcos pointed to the source a moment later. Ella and Mikael leaned heavily on each other while Chadwick swung a barstool behind them as they fled a group of bloodied dancers. Filigrees of electric magic ran from Chadwick's hands down through the barstool and sparkled at the end of the legs, where they fizzled out.

"It's Sera's friends," he whispered. "We can't leave them to the cannibals."

"Potential cannibals," Taneisha enthusiastically corrected from behind us, as if by metaphorically underlining the word that the cannibals would be less threatening.

"We can't leave Sera's family to fend for themselves," Caden added. "We have to bring them with us."

I nodded in agreement. "Looks like their magic is fading, and they're running out of time. Ideas for distractions?"

"I could shift and make some noise," Marcos offered.

"I hate to break it to you, but panthers don't fare well against raving Dionysian revelers," Caden added.

Marcos' brows shot up. "Oh, yeah, on second thought..."

"I say we brute force it," Caden continued. "Rush in, rush out."

"I can help!" Taneisha said, tapping a thoughtful finger against her lips. "I'll blind them with a menagerie of butterflies!"

"Do it," I replied to the fae, beyond questioning her motivations at this moment, just grateful for the help. Then I tapped into the energy of Velvet, made chaotic by Taneisha's magic, aiming to amp up the music and lights on the dance floor. After a moment, Velvet responded with a bone-jarring bass beat. Not quite what I'd hoped for, but it was something. "Let's go," I called out over the noise.

Marcos led the charge, with Caden and I following on his heels. Chadwick and Mikael stood between the cannibals and Ella, backing up as the cannibals closed in around them. I ducked as a roar of fluttering wings passed by overhead, rolling out over the gardens, forming a visual wall between us and most of the cannibals.

When we reached the trio, I could tell they wouldn't have held out much longer on their own. Marcos yelled and punched the closest bloodied reveler, knocking them down onto their ass. A red-eyed Caden kicked another square in the gut, sending them flying backward into a host of butterflies. I pulled a bloody raver away from Mikael, punching them square in the jaw.

I grabbed Chadwick by the arm. "Let's go!"

The three needed no more encouragement. Marcos swept up a limping Ella and carried her. Caden helped Mikael, who held tight to his side, his face a mask of pain. I led us back to the hidden cave, glancing back to see the revelers distracted by swooping butterflies and the loud music coming from the dance floor.

I pulled back the vines, gesturing for Chadwick to enter.

He held back. "What's on the other side?"

"It's not here?" I replied.

"That's not much of an endorsement," Ella replied as Marcos set her down on her feet.

"Are you okay?" Caden asked Mikael.

"I think I broke a rib or two." Mikael winced. "But Ella twisted her ankle. Where's Sera and your other friends?"

"We're finding them next. That cave's headed the same direction we last saw her going," Marcos replied, his tone so full of bluster even I believed him. "I think I know where we can find a medical kit with gear to stabilize

Ella's ankle on the way, too. But we need to keep moving and stay ahead of the cannibals."

"Potential cannibals," Taneisha added, earning herself an eye roll from Ella.

"So, you don't know if Sera's okay?" Chadwick asked, his tone an indictment.

"She's fine," I said. "Em and Liam should be with her by now, too."

"I'm not inclined to trust any of you," Chadwick replied.

"You're welcome to stay here. Your choice," I said.

Caden led the way down the tunnel. Sera's friends followed, although Chadwick glowered my way before stepping into the tunnel.

I grabbed Marcos' shoulder before he followed, holding him back. "For all the crazy nights we've seen at Velvet, I've always relied on you to have my back, brother. I don't know how I'd manage without you."

He grinned. "You wouldn't, so I'm not about to leave you to figure it out on your own. Now come on." Marcos disappeared into the cave after the others.

Taneisha stepped close to me, her shrewd gaze lingering on my bloodied knuckles. "I can see what Sera likes about your cadre. You're all so gallant." She spit out the last word like an insult. "Although you are fraying about the edges now, aren't you, golden-haired boy?"

"I'm not the one who turned Velvet into a dumpster fire," I shot back. "This is not my mess."

She shrugged me off, gazing out at the gardens. "Don't you think it's a little funny that the demi-god of madness and revelry is the one who can't cope when the shit, or in this case, the blood, hits the fan?"

"I'm coping just fine," I said, wishing the words to be true, but my gut flip-flopped as I followed the fae's gaze.

Taneisha arched her brow. "Are you though?"

How long would it take me to set things to rights here? How would I handle the injuries and damages Taneisha had caused? She'd wanted to hurt me, and she'd succeeded, but I didn't back down. "All the injuries here are on your head. You may want to punish us, but can you live with the harm you've caused?"

She chewed her lip before answering, a crack forming in her fearless, hard-hearted fae facade. "You sound like Ray."

"Ray? You mean the minotaur, Raymond?" Why would she bring him up?

"Never you mind." Taneisha waved me off. "You'd better catch up with your boys and your mage, Franc," she deflected. "Go on, move along then."

"You're not coming with us?" I asked. Not that I cared, other than I almost preferred to keep an eye on what the fae was up to. Yeah, that was it. I certainly couldn't be worried about the fae and how she might manage against a crowd of potential cannibals. Not after all Taneisha had pulled.

Could I?

Taneisha flagged me away with her hands. "Ew, no. I'm too busy to hang out with mages, shifters, and demi-gods. Or your stinking shifter bros. No, no, thank you." She flicked her fingers, opened a portal, and marched off through it without another word.

DRUNK THE MILK OF PARADISE

SERA

I couldn't quite remember how I'd found this paradise, but I knew I never wanted to leave. I hadn't felt this vibrant and alive... well ever. Flowers sprung from the ground with every step. Fountains of wine gurgled. The air was crisp and clear, beckoning me to adventure. I could lift boulders and the ground shook when I hit the ground with my staff. Everywhere I looked, people celebrated life with such abandon and joy.

I'd found bliss.

Yet, something unsettled snaked through the back of my mind. I narrowed my gaze, trying to remember where I was. It was a curious, expansive space full of black leather furniture and odd wooden devices with chains and cuffs at the ready. Vines had taken over latticework panels, serving as living partitions between spaces. Sections of the concrete floor heaved upward as life invaded and order yielded to nature. In another area, the concrete floor had dropped away, giving ground to a vast goldfish-filled pool covering the far end of the room. Even my staff had caught life, sprouting oak leaves along the top section as if it, too, would fight back against death itself.

Why had I come here? Hadn't I been doing something? Something important?

And why was that person covered in blood? Or was it wine? Here, the fountains flowed with seemingly endless draughts.

A raucous round of "Huzzah!" and "Io! Evohe!" shouts echoed through the hall and off the black-painted walls. I joined in, thumping the ground with my staff and hearing my voice rattle the legs of furniture against the concrete.

These were my people. This was where I belonged.

I looked around for a cup, and finding none, I picked up a chunk of loose concrete from the floor. I envisioned the shape of the cup inside the block and called forth my desires. Dust and chunks fell away, leaving me with a stone goblet, which I dunked into a fountain of wine and then raised to my lips. The rich liquid coated my tongue, its liquid heat soothing my spirit.

"Hunt! Hunt! Hunt!" The calls filtered through the crowd, captivating me. This was new. Celebratory cheers rang out, and I knew they'd captured their quarry.

"Bring it to me!" I declared, eager to see what my people had captured.

Multiple whoops answered my proclamation, and soon they deposited two bundles at my feet, each wrapped in pale pink silk and covered in dirt and blood. One of them groaned and moved, while the other did not.

"We caught them nosing around at the doors, o' powerful one," a raver announced, bowing low.

I set aside my staff and wine and then bent down over the bundles. I pulled the fabric away, revealing the two men within. There was something familiar about them, but I couldn't quite place it. Both had close-cut beards, but while one was pale and rough, the other struck me as sun struck, polished, and refined. The pale one had bruising down the side of his face and his breath was shallow. Had they injured him? The very thought angered me beyond reason.

The one with the golden-kissed skin opened his deep brown eyes, his gaze falling immediately to me. My breath caught in my throat as his sizzling intensity rolled over me. I luxuriated in the heat, feeling my body warm to his presence. Surely, I knew him, but from where?

"Here you are. We need to go," he said, then groaned as he rolled onto his side and kicked the makeshift bag off. "We have to find the others."

"There's nothing lost, traveler. I'm right where I belong," I replied, hearing the power in my words. "And so are you."

He hesitated then, as if realizing he was out of his depth. His gaze caught on his friend, and he tensed. "Liam!" He reached over and placed his hands on the other's chest and head, and then appeared to pray.

I reclaimed my wine and sipped, fascinated by our new arrivals. They weren't animals, or we'd feast. Still, I couldn't let them alter our plans.

After a minute, the bruised one coughed and opened his eyes, looking as bewildered as his friend had a few moments prior.

"What happened?" Liam asked.

"You got knocked over the head and they captured us. Luckily, they brought us straight to Sera."

He looked at me then, and I realized he was referring

to me. Was I Sera? The name struck a chord, but it felt far away, as if from another life. Another time.

Liam pushed himself up, wincing as he moved. He took in the crowd, his gaze wary. "Are you okay? Did they hurt you?" he asked me.

"Hurt me?" I laughed, the sound of my voice carrying to the far corners of this room. "I am invincible here. No one is fool enough to try me."

The two shared a dubious look, and I didn't like the look of it. Of them.

"We should find Franc and the others, Sera," said the brown-eyed one, rising to his feet. "They're looking for us."

"Should?" I asked, incredulous at the suggestion. How dare he tell me what to do? How to be? "If these others look," I spread my arms wide, "they shall find. All roads lead to this sanctuary, and I welcome them."

Liam pulled himself to his feet, although he was a little unsteady, no doubt from that nasty bump on his head. "Em?" he asked the other one, and I understood that to be his friend's name.

"Perhaps we should get Franc?" Em asked.

"I'm not leaving her here," Liam replied.

I refilled my wine glass as the two talked. It was almost like they didn't think I, or my revelers, could hear them.

"Me neither. What are you proposing?" Em asked.

Liam planted his hands on his hips. "We need to convince Sera to come with us somehow."

I arched a brow at that statement and then drank down my cup.

"They have some sort of hold over her," Em added. "Perhaps she'll recognize our touch?"

"Enough. I think you need some time to come to your

senses, lads," I said. "Chain them up," I decreed, and my ravers moved at once in accordance with my will.

The newcomers tried to fight them off, but they were only two, while my revelers were many. Before long, my people had dragged them off and chained them up on some nearby conveniently located trusses. I took a perch on a bench across from these outsiders as I considered their fate. Surely, they would benefit from joining us.

"What the hells is this room?" Liam asked, fighting against his chains. "Or what was it before Taneisha got her claws into it?"

"It's Velvet's premier BDSM room," Em replied. He seemed much more resigned to his captivity. "Or at least it was before a group of raving bacchants converted it to a wine jungle with a pool."

"Thus, the ample supply of chains," Liam replied, pulling against his in a way I found provocative. "What's our next move?"

"We have to reach her," Em said, his gaze never leaving me.

He was filled with such a sizzling hunger for life. A girl could get lost in those eyes of his.

"I should have bitten you when I had the chance," Liam spat out. "I could shift and break free, and then I'd prove to you where you belong. Our mating bond will snap you out of this thrall of madness."

"Bite me?" I laughed. I couldn't help but wonder at his phrasing or what he meant. There was something familiar about all of this, but I couldn't bring the memories to the surface of my mind. "Even if you broke free, we'd just tie you up again. And I know where I belong. You belong here too."

"You're half right on that. Come here and I'll show you," he dared me.

Fearless, I strode up to the wild-eyed man, animalistic energy pouring off him in waves. I leaned in close, thrilling at the feel of his body pressed against mine. There was a familiarity with how we fit together. He sniffed along my neck, and my skin prickled, as if every cell in my body was alive and on fire for him.

"You can't," Em said, emotion strangling his voice. "She can't consent, and Sera will never forgive you when she comes to her senses. Neither will the rest of us, if you take advantage of her in this state."

"You got a better idea?" Liam ground out between clenched teeth.

"I do," I interrupted their irritating banter, holding up my wine cup to Liam's lips. "You drink, and then I'll let you bite me."

The look of yearning, of raw hunger, in his eyes stole my breath away.

"Just drink," I urged. "Then you can have whatever else you need."

Em was nearly frothing at the mouth. "I swear by all the gods, Liam, if you do this, I will kick your ass, heal it, and then kick it again."

Liam nodded, and I poured the wine into his mouth, bringing him into my revelers.

THE DEN OF INIQUITY

FRANC

"Explain to me again what the plan is?" Chadwick asked.

We'd somehow made it through the cave and into the basement without running into any more ravers, and now hunkered down in an alcove off the hallway leading to one of the more remote areas of Velvet. Marcos had located a first aid kit and was bandaging up Ella's ankle while we stopped to plan our next move. From the noise coming out of the hall leading to the Den, I knew where our maenad Sera had led the revelers.

"I walk into the Den of Iniquity and confront Sera head on. Only I can bring her back from this madness," I explained. "Afterward, we'll get Liam and Emrys, and then together we can head back to the dance floor and work together to free my mask from the fae's magical knot."

"Why is the room called the Den of Iniquity?" Ella asked.

"It's the BDSM room, so..." Caden explained.

"These cannibals are with Sera in there?" Ella asked.

"That's extra kinky." As the pitch of her siren's voice climbed with every word, her externalized anxiety grated on my nerves.

"You say only you can save her, but it sounds like you caused this whole mess," Chadwick replied. "I think we need a better plan than just you walk in and talk her out past the masses of unstable ravers."

"I'm telling you, this is the only way," I said.

"I disagree. Mages stick with mages," Chadwick replied. "It's our custom."

I suspected he also meant mages usually only dated other mages, but he didn't say it. I wanted to point out not only was I a demi-god of Dionysos, but Caden, Marcos, and I were also Sera's mates, damn the rules. We were the ones she needed now, but it seemed like a bad time to break that news to her cousin and friends.

"This is my club. Mine. Maenads and bacchantes are my purview, not mage business," I insisted. I refrained from declaring just how much Sera's safety was my business, not theirs. "I just need your help to distract the ravers while I get through to Sera."

"What did you have in mind?" Mikael asked.

Thank goodness one of them was level-headed.

"There's a sound and video booth that covers the Den accessible from the far end of the hall. Caden and Marcos will get you there safely. Once you have control of the sound system, Ella can calm all the ravers using her siren's gifts with no risk to yourselves."

"You want me to sing cannibalistic ravers to sleep?" Ella asked.

"They were human first," I pointed out. "Can't sirens

enchant people, even when they're experiencing altered states?"

"Yeah. I can give it a shot," Ella replied.

Mikael huffed out a breath. "What's our back-up plan if you're not able to get Sera out of there?"

"I'll get her out." When they just stared, I shrugged. "If I can't talk her out, then I'll grab her, and we run."

"You sure you want to go in there alone?" Marcos asked me.

No, I didn't. But I'd rather only have to drag Sera and myself past the revelers.

"If I need you, you'll hear me."

Caden clapped me on the shoulder. "We've got your back. Now get in there and knock em dead!"

I trusted Caden and Marcos. I wasn't sure at all about Sera's cousin and her friends, but we were low on options. We hadn't run into Liam or Emrys on the way here, so they couldn't help us now.

I ran a hand through my curls and headed into the hallway. I hoped, as the lineage of Dionysos, that I still had some level of control over the mayhem I'd find inside. Something the fae's magic hadn't yet turned against me. "Likely not the best phrasing, demon," I called back behind me.

"We're not doing phrasing anymore?" Caden replied, a wide grin on his face.

I let out a weak laugh as I headed down the corridor. Damn him, but I loved how Caden made me laugh even at the most serious of times.

The noise of the ravers amplified as I neared the doorway at the end of the hall and I tuned my senses to the madness within. I was no stranger to bacchanals and orgiastic revelry, but the energy emanating from the Den tripped well beyond dancing on the edge of madness. Under the wild bent of Taneisha's fae energy warping my own, the ravers had danced right up to that edge, stomped on the boundary of sanity, and rushed off into the untamed spaces beyond reason.

Luckily, I was uniquely suited not just at walking people to the edge so they could blow off some steam, but at drawing them back down before anyone got hurt. I might be late to the party, but I had every faith in my powers and their ability to bring calm to the storm.

I could only hope Sera wasn't beyond my reach.

I stepped into the room and paused, feeling a wave of unsettling energy wash over me. It did not surprise me to find a trio of ravers watching the door, as if expecting my arrival. The light was dim in the space, but I couldn't miss how trees and vines had erupted through the floor and grown high into the ceiling, transforming the Den into a de facto forest.

And was that a lake at the far end?

Definitely not how I'd left it. The list of things I'd have to clean up got longer with every room in Velvet I entered. It wasn't lost on me how, off all the legacy quests, Taneisha had delivered the biggest headaches my way.

Of course.

A woman clothed in tattered clothing, wine, and blood moved to meet me. "Greetings, walker of the wine-dark earth. I will take you to the ivy-bearer."

By the gods...

"Lead on," I replied. I followed the woman through a circuitous path. We passed many revelers, most of whom didn't even look up or take notice of us. Perhaps I should have done more to help all of them, but right now, my worries were for Sera alone. I had to save my energy for pulling her out of this mess.

"Drink, drink, drink!" came a chant from up ahead. When we rounded a curve in the path and entered a clearing, the first thing I saw was Sera pouring wine down Liam's throat as the ravers urged them on. They'd cuffed both Liam and Emrys up side by side on a pair of St. Andrews crosses, no doubt at Sera's will. She still wore the swath of pink silk tied around her like a toga that I'd seen her wearing as she left the temple. It'd gained a few stains and didn't leave a hell of a lot to the imagination, but she didn't appear to mind.

When she turned to me, I felt the connection between us snap taut like a wire. She lowered the wineglass and took a step back from Liam, before she stalked toward me. Liam threw his head back and howled, his guttural roar empowered by wine-drenched madness. Ravers howled along in solidarity with Liam, but I kept my focus on my mate.

"Thank the gods you got here just in time," Emrys exclaimed, sagging against his chains in relief. "Liam was about to bite Sera. He thinks claiming her will break her out of this madness."

"Well, timing is everything." I pondered Emrys' words. Was Liam right? Would claiming Sera as our mate release her from the magic's hold upon her?

Sera stopped before me; her eyes lit with an inner fire. Or was it a tinge of insanity?

"Wine god," she greeted me.

"Maenad," I replied.

"So you have marked me, lord of the frenzy."

The last thing I needed was to follow Sera down into this rabbit hole of madness. "I'll pass for now. And I didn't mark you, Sera. I opened a door, but you were the one to run through it."

She arched a brow and then leaned in close. "Tell yourself whatever you like, god-born. You branded me with your power. This isn't just a door you can close and pretend nothing happened."

Sera's words sunk in, and I wondered at the consequences of our time in the temple together. I'd wanted to free her. Release her from Taneisha's magic. Had my push of magic marked her as well?

It's not like there was a manual to god mates. At least, not one that I'd been given.

I heard the sound system click on, followed by a gradual fade in of a leisurely Mozart sonata. The ravers didn't give any sign of noticing anything amiss, if the naked oil wrestling match going on behind those ferns was any sign.

She held up the glass. "Thirsty?"

When I didn't answer, she shrugged and downed the rest of her beverage before tossing her cup to the floor, where it shattered into bits.

I reached out and tucked a wild lock of hair behind her ear. "You're magnificent."

"It's easy when you're awesome. I didn't know I could feel this comfortable with my magic. The power is endless."

Sera puckered her wine-stained lips, and I longed to swoop her into my arms and have a taste, but I knew I had to handle this conversation delicately, or Sera might have me chained up to a cross next.

The sound of Ella's lilting voice added to the Mozart, quiet enough that I couldn't quite make out the words, but the tune reminded me of a children's lullaby. Even at low volume, I felt her siren's magic in the notes, calming me. The background noise of the room slowly diminished, so I knew it was influencing the revelers as well.

I placed my hand at the crux of her neck and shoulder, pulling Sera close to me. Her eyes fluttered as Ella's music blunted the edge of Sera's madness.

I let my magic flow out and over Sera, hooking into the madness flowing beneath her skin. I reined in her wine-drenched power, feeling it slowly diminish as I funneled it deep down into the earth. As I grounded out Sera's energy, the rest of the room calmed as well, as if they were all feeding off her state. I wasn't sure if it would last with the revelers, but as Sera's eyes cleared, I knew she was coming back to earth. Some revelers near us sank to the ground, and I knew the tide was turning in our favor.

"You are awesome, my mage turned maenad. An inspiration, truly. But right now, I need my mage back." She opened her mouth to argue, but I cut her off. "This state, this intensity, it's for visiting. It's not meant to last."

But as her clarity returned, Sera's bliss state faded. She looked around us, now shocked at the blooded revelers.

"What are you doing, Franc?" she asked, panic etching her features as her mind cleared.

"It's just a little nap. I don't even think it'll last long once Ella stops signing."

"Oh, my. I remember all of this. And that," she said, pointing to Liam and Emrys. Emrys waved. Liam had fallen asleep.

"You'll be fine, although the energy hangover can be a doozy," I explained.

Sera cocked her head to the side, and her gaze narrowed on me. "Wait. I won't let you do this."

"I told you," I reassured her, "these things aren't meant to last."

"Explain it to me," she demanded.

I felt her power rising again under the surface. Sera reached out her hand and called her staff to her. It flew toward her, and she caught it with strength and grace, pounding it down with a force that vibrated the ground. The resonance reverberated, and a moment later, the cuffs on Emrys and Liam clicked, falling open. Emrys went to Liam, who'd slumped sleepily to the ground under the influence of Ella's siren lullabies.

"You pushed me to this state for a reason. You marked me with your powers. Why?"

I hesitated for only a moment. "I wanted you to let loose. I hoped you'd gain new control over your powers through the transcendence of madness."

"Uh huh," Sera shook her head. "You may have wanted me to 'evolve,'" she used air quotes. "But you didn't just push me to see what I would become. Sure, you wanted me to embrace my powers. Free me from Taneisha' geas. But also, you need me, all of us really, strong enough to save your legacy. Not to mention your precious Velvet."

Silence rang through in the air as the truth of her words hit me square in the gut. Emrys glowered in my direction, but didn't interrupt us, even though I wished he'd diffuse the tension between us.

"Tell me I'm wrong," she pressed.

"I can't," I admitted. "I'm sorry. I shouldn't have

pushed you. At the time, I didn't even question my motives."

"Thank you." Sera sighed. "You marked me, Franc. That's not cool, but we'll deal with that later. There was a need you felt, even if you didn't consciously understand it, and you acted on it."

"There is truth in madness," I explained. "Madness is the answer I've fallen back on time and time again."

She nodded; eyes filled with empathy despite her ire. "Take a moment and then tell me. What are you fighting for? Velvet? Your legacy mask? Me?"

I laughed, running a hand through my hair to distract myself from the discomfort of the moment. "Can't it be all three?"

"That's a cop out if I've ever heard one. So, what's your plan?" Sera asked, but she kept right on going. "Was the plan seriously just to get the gang back together and then rush in there throwing magic, shifters, and siren songs around? Maybe the rest of us can hold back the tide of bloody cannibals while Franc solves the puzzle?"

Emrys had revived Liam, and the two moved closer to us, but didn't interrupt.

"I mean, that's what I was thinking," I replied, but my words sounded dubious even as I uttered them.

"And why do you believe you can solve the knot's puzzle now, and not either of the two prior times?"

My thoughts focused with sudden clarity. "Because it's not about forcing my way through. It's about respecting the process, the pattern, so I can work with it and not against it. At least I think so?"

Sera leaned in and pressed her forehead against mine.

"That's better than what you had before. Now I think you have a shot."

"Where does this leave us?" I whispered. "I can't lose you, Sera."

Sera took a deep breath and then stepped away. "I can't predict tomorrow's problems, but right now, you've got a fae puzzle to solve. You best get to it."

"What are you going to do?"

"I'm gonna pied piper my bloodied revelers into a proper shindig somewhere other than the dance floor. Speaking of." Sera pounded her staff on the ground, and the revelers Ella had lulled to sleep awoke, groaning and moaning.

"Quickly!" she exclaimed, pointing her staff towards the exit. "Flee while you can."

WHEN THE GOING GETS TOUGH, THE TOUGH ROLL WITH THE REVELERS

FRANC

Emrys, Liam, and I fled the Den of Iniquity, rejoining the others in the hallway outside.

"Follow us," I said.

"Isn't Sera coming?" Chadwick asked. "We saw you talking but couldn't hear what you discussed."

"She's going to create a distraction," Emrys replied. "But we need to stay ahead of her."

"And the ravers," Liam added.

The chanting of the revelers behind us in the Den was enough to convince everyone to keep moving. We ran back down the basement halls, through the cave, and emerged once more in the gardens. Only then did we take a few moments to whisper amongst ourselves.

"Why did you tell Sera to romp through the hills with zombie bacchants?" Chadwick sneered. "She should be here with us."

"I'd think you'd know no one commands Sera," I replied. "And they aren't zombies. They're cannibals."

"What?!?" Ella yelled, and Mikael shushed her.

"Not so loud," he whispered. "You'll draw unwanted attention."

"But you said cannibals?" Ella said to me. "Seriously?"

"Sometimes when bacchants get a little wild, they lose control and experiment with flesh-eating. I haven't seen it happen before, but I've heard stories from my grandpa," I explained.

"How is that better?" Ella asked. "That's still cannibalism."

"It just is?" I scrubbed a hand across my face. Wasn't it? "Look, we need to get moving. Once I free my mask, the fae's spell keeping us locked in here ends."

"Nope. There's no way I'm going out there with those cannibal zombies running around!" Ella replied.

"Flesh eat…" I started to reply.

"Nope!" she whispered way too loudly.

"Fine," Emrys replied. "Stay here and wait for us then. But we can't guarantee your safety."

"Like you can out there?" she bit back.

Ella had a point, and Sera wouldn't want him to place her family and friends at undue risk. "You're right, this is going to be dangerous. You should stay here. It's secluded."

"No, we're stronger together," Mikael replied. Ella shot him a look of frustration, but he pulled her to him. "Think about it, Ella. If Franc doesn't crack that knot, how much longer will the fae trap us here? We'd be trading momentary safety and comfort for greater risk later."

Hearing Mikael's strategic thinking and bravery, he truly sounded like her kin.

While waiting for Ella to reply, Chadwick spoke up. "Sera trusts them, for whatever reason. I suppose that's good enough for me. I'm with you both," he said to Ella and Mikael, "whatever you decide."

"Ugh, fine," Ella conceded. "We haven't even been in here for a day and I can't take it anymore. So, what's the plan?"

As if in response, a mighty whooping and hollering erupted from the temple, followed by a steady stream of revelers rushing out into the garden. At the forefront Sera led the pack, her pink toga trailing out behind her like a war banner, bloody stains stark against the lush fabric. Her eyes burned with an inner fire that never seemed to fail her.

"Sera will draw people out from the dance floor," I said. "Once they've thinned out, we move in and you all hold off the remaining revelers while I solve that damned knot."

The throng chanted, and we listened with rapt attention to their words.

> *Dionysos, god of wine and ecstasy,*
> *Come to us in your bacchic revelry.*
> *Bring us joy and abandon,*
> *Let us dance and sing all night.*
>
> *Your Maenads follow you,*
> *Entranced by your wild beauty.*
> *They dance and they sing,*
> *They make love in the forest.*
>
> *You lead us to ecstasy,*
> *You teach us to let go.*
> *In your arms, we are free,*
> *And we know only pleasure.*

So come to us now,
Dionysos, god of wine and ecstasy.
Bring us joy and abandon,
Let us dance and sing all night.

The ravers circled through the garden, repeating the lines from their song as they moved in a circle around Sera, who stood atop a short stone wall pounding her staff upon the rock like a metronome.

"There they go," Marcos added, pointing to the revelers exiting the dance hall. "That's our cue. Everyone stay close to the wall on our left and stick to the shadows where you can."

If Marcos expected us to behave with military precision, he'd be disappointed. I led the way with Caden at my side, noticing that Marcos remained in the rear with Emrys and Liam, perhaps thinking they could shield us all from the hordes if necessary.

"Don't look now, but your remodel budget just blew out," Caden said to me.

Now I had to look. Groups of ravers were knocking down statues and ripping limbs off the cedar trees. I groaned. "I can worry about remodeling Velvet some other time. Right now, I just need to save all of us," I replied.

"And your mask. And your revelers," Caden replied. "Simple."

I stopped up short, bringing our line to a halt. "No, Caden. The mask is secondary to liberating everyone here."

Caden's expression softened. "Of course, I'm just giving

you a ration of shit, Franc. C'mon, we've got partying cannibals depending on us."

"Right," I replied, shaking my head at his dark humor. "Sorry, there's just so much on the line. So many people Taneisha hurt with her revenge."

Caden nodded. "I know, man. We're almost there and the club looks mostly cleared out."

I led us into the club, using my now limited influence over Velvet to lower the blaring music as we entered. I strode to the center of the room where my mask remained locked inside the knot of magical vines. The others fanned out around me, forming a physical shield against the ravers who even now were filtering back into the room like moths to a flame.

Taneisha had made it clear only I could solve this puzzle. The weight of this moment laid heavy on my shoulders, but I knew I was up to the challenge. I walked up to the box and took a deep breath to center myself before I started. The last time I'd made some progress pulling apart the vines, but they were living things, and when one had loosened, another had tightened. Taneisha had designed this puzzle for me, so I had to imagine that it was possible for me to solve.

Was I going about this entirely the wrong way?

"Looks like we're getting a steady stream of revelers coming back in. They aren't getting close yet," Marcos said. "No pressure."

I tried to ignore the growing noise in the room. I picked at the vines, but again, they fought me. I tore and ripped at them, but that didn't work either. For every vine I ripped away, another appeared in its place.

What was I supposed to do to make this work?

Then I thought of the vines and how they moved as if alive. Like they were rooted to the column below them. Perhaps fiddling with the vines directly wasn't workable. Perhaps I had to go to the source.

I took hold of the cage, put one foot upon the column for leverage, and pulled with all my might. For a moment nothing happened, but then the structure gave way and separated from the column all at once, sending the stone column topping to the floor. When it hit, the stone shattered, flying in all directions.

I held the cage as it undulated between my hands, as if might escape me, but I held on.

"Nice trick, what now?" Liam asked.

"I'm not sure," I said. As I looked over the cage for new weaknesses, I noticed its movements were slowing. In less than a minute, the vines were withering and browning. "Wait, I think we're good after all. The vines are dying."

"You did it!" Emrys declared.

Everyone turned to watch as the vines turned to husks and fell apart under my hands. Soon all I held was the mask, and I clutched it to my chest in relief.

Taneisha appeared, slowly clapping as she walked across the dance floor toward us. "Congratulations, Franc, you've won back your grandpa's divine god mask. Huzzah! Too bad your revelers damaged your club just a wee bit before you solved the puzzle."

"Damaged? It's trashed. This is going to take months to set back to rights."

"Can we just call it collateral damage? Friendly fire?"

I didn't take the bait. Little would be accomplished by arguing semantics with Taneisha. "Free everyone," I demanded. "And heal them. Now."

The fae arched a brow at my tone, but snapped her fingers, releasing her hold on Velvet. The sensation washed over me, and I breathed a sigh of relief knowing the nightmare was over. Sera strode into the dance hall, still clothed in her makeshift toga and carrying her staff. I wondered how long she'd be carrying that around. The ravers inside the dance hall looked around in confusion, as if they'd just awoken from a deep sleep.

"I freed your revelers and healed them, but they'll remain in a fog until they get a good night's rest. They will remember this trial as a nightmare," she said, dramatically pouting her lips. "Sadly, I doubt many will return to partake in future festivities."

When Sera reached us, it was obvious she'd heard Taneisha's words. "We need to stay and help these people," Sera said. "Unless you're offering to manage healing them and getting them back to their homes?" she asked the fae.

Taneisha threw her hands in the air like she was helpless to assist further. "I healed them. What else do you want? Oh right, it's time for your last quest," Taneisha announced. "Stay and help these flesh-eating revelers, and you refuse the call and lose the opportunity to rescue Emrys' legacy forever."

EPILOGUE - A CLAIM STAKED

SERA

Taneisha opened a portal before us, and I could see her familiar green fairy glen on the other side. From the unenthusiastic looks on my posse's faces, no one was ready yet for another roll of the dice fae quest.

"We'll go, but we can't leave these people to their own devices," I insisted. "They're stumbling around like zombies."

"Flesh eaters," Ella whispered my way.

Caden cracked up, and it was clear I'd missed an inside joke.

"You're on the clock, my maenad with the mostest. My clock," Taneisha continued. "No time to dawdle. You've got another puzzle to solve."

Although the maenad madness had faded when Taneisha had dropped the magic holding everyone trapped in the club, I still felt vestiges of the power imprinted upon me. Franc's power. I glanced at Franc, still unsure of how to feel about what he'd done. What he'd pushed me into being. I didn't know how long the effects would last, but I found I liked the energy shift. It felt like the Dionysian energy complemented my mage powers, and I didn't know what to make of that.

Then there was the scrap of silk I'd made into a toga. I mean, I was practically walking around naked, and now that everyone had their wits about them again, including me, I wanted to find something more substantial. Pronto. I was totally ready for one of Taneisha's trademark wardrobe changes.

"We'll stay and help," Mikael offered. "Between Ella, Chadwick, and myself, we can stay and get everyone home safely."

"Thank you," I replied.

"Yeah, how could we not?" Chadwick replied. "But there's one condition."

My stomach flip-flopped. We hadn't parted on the best of terms. When my magic had gone chaotic, I'd broken things off with a dramatic argument. It hadn't been my finest moment. "What do you want?"

It was Mikael who answered. "If I go home and tell my mom that I saw you and didn't drag you straight back to Ms. Lowe, she might make my clothes itch like poison ivy for a week straight."

"That's oddly specific and definitely something we all want you to avoid," I replied. "What would you do if she did that? Stay home naked the entire time?"

"Yeah, pretty much," Mikael chuckled. "I need an explanation that my mom and Ms. Lowe will accept."

I looked around at my guys, each of whom waited to see what I'd say. I couldn't explain all of it, but I could stick to the truth. Mostly.

"Tell them I took a job for Emrys Tedros that involves his close friends and the fae Taneisha. There's one more step in the job to complete, and then I'll report in with granny. It won't take over three more days?" I shot a look at Taneisha, who wobbled her hand in front of her, and then held up four fingers. "All right, four more days. You can also tell granny I'm fine. Taneisha has guaranteed my safety."

I left out the relationship entanglements, and mating claims, that had come up between me and the posse. I could only hope Mikael would leave what he'd seen out of his explanation.

Mikael shook his head. "There's no way in hells I'm calling her granny. I can't even repeat that you called her granny."

I laughed. "But she'd treat you to her famous imperious stare!"

"That isn't all she'd do," he muttered, and then turned to Taneisha. "Is that true, fae? Speak plainly and tell me you guarantee my cousin's safety."

Taneisha smiled the sweetest of smiles. Almost too sweet. "I swear, Seraphina Lowe will return safely home after completing the quests. I will not allow any harm to come to Sera."

Definitely too sweet.

Hearing the fae's saccharine promise, I immediately distrusted her. Fae were bound to their word, and I couldn't see a way around her statement. By the frowns of the others, I could tell I wasn't the only one not buying her act, but it would have to do.

"Okay then, that's at least something. Take care of yourself, and you five," he pointed at each of the posse. "If anything happens to Sera, nothing will save you from the Lowe clan taking it out of your hides."

"Heard, mage," Liam replied. "We will not fail in our duty to Sera."

"I don't doubt you, wolf," Chadwick replied. "But after seeing what Taneisha will do to put you through for her games, well, you need all the luck that you can get."

"Can you all see me right now?" Taneisha asked. "Cause you're talking like you don't."

There were some awkward stares back and forth, but no one responded.

"Fine then, enough with the goodbyes. We're on a schedule." Taneisha pointed to her still-open portal. "Last one through's a wet noodle!"

We all hesitated.

"Not literally, right?" Franc asked.

Taneisha laughed with abandon. "No, silly, not literally. Or is that figuratively? I'm never sure. I just mean, you're all dragging your heels and it's killing my momentum."

We let out a collective breath.

"Off we go," Marcos said, heading toward the portal. "We've had swamps, mazes, even hell. What is it this time?" he asked over his shoulder. "An ice planet?"

"I'm turning up the heat, baby!" Taneisha replied. "This time, in honor of Emrys' heritage, we're going to the desert!"

"Oh joy," Caden said, following Marcos. "At least demons can take the heat."

"Less so for shifters," Liam added, following on Caden's heels, "but we'll make do."

Emrys and Franc appeared to be waiting for me, but I motioned them through with my staff. They seemed dubious, especially Emrys, but went ahead. I walked up to Taneisha, facing off with her next to the portal.

"You got a place where I can store this?" I held up my staff.

She winked. "You know I do."

"Also, I know you usually have plans for our wardrobe, but I have some ideas," I said.

"Why didn't you say something sooner? Whatever you want, you know it's no problem at all. Can I just say, this ensemble you have going on right now, it's so 'goddess of destruction who isn't taking your shit' vibes? I love it!"

"I know, right?"

I glanced back at Chadwick, Ella, and Mikael, who all appeared to be battling differing stages of anxiety.

I shot them a quick queen wave and a smile and then I turned and walked through the portal with Taneisha at my side. "Here's what I'm thinking."

THE END

Thank you so much for reading Reckless Rapture! It would mean a lot to me if you could leave a review. A single line or two makes a big difference for other people when deciding if a book is a good fit for them.

Want a bonus epilogue? Download more of the story as newsletter exclusive content!
https://geni.us/HiddenHeartsBonus

The next book in the series, Sworn Spirits, is available for preorder now.

Four legacies down, one to go. Angry with Franc for pressing his claim on me, I grab Emrys and rush headlong into the next challenge, leaving the others minutes behind us.

Turns out, when you're stuck in a magical faery time loop, moments matter.

I used to fear angering the fae Taneisha, but after battling my way through so many of her mind games, illusions, and tricks, I'm over her so-called amusements. Over her. All we have to do is find Emrys's golden scorpion, and then everything can finally get back to normal for all six of us.

Right?

Who am I kidding? After our time together at Franc's club Velvet, is normal even possible? Could I really go back to quiet days running my coffee shop, before the posse re-entered my life? After all we've been through, I can't bear to think of leaving them behind. With each repeat of time through the fae's loop, I see another potential future. Another spin of the wheel of fate.

Hunting through the oppressive desert heat has everyone's nerves at a breaking point, bringing out all our heightened emotions. Can we time everything just right to escape Taneisha's machinations, retrieve the golden scorpion, and repair our frayed bonds?

ALSO BY CANDICE BUNDY

The Stolen Legacy Series

Forbidden Fates

Entangled Essence

Hidden Hearts

Reckless Rapture

Sworn Spirits

The Shadow Series

Shadow in the City, A prequel novella

Twinned Shadow

Poisoned Shadow

Shadow Underground

Caught Between Worlds Series

Smoke and Daemons

(previously published as Daemon Whisperer)

Other Works

Ripples, a novella

Open Rack, a contemporary short

~

WRITING AS CR BUNDY

The Depths of Memory Series

The Dream Sifter

Dreams Manifest

For a list of my full catalog of available titles, visit my
candicebundy.com/books page.

ALSO BY PIPER FOX

Academy for Reapers: Paranormal Romance

Big Wolf on Campus Series: Wolf Shifter Football Romances

The Stolen Legacy Series: Paranormal Reverse Harem

Midnight Huntress Series: Paranormal Reverse Harem

Alien Warriors of New Dilaria Series: Sci-Fi Reverse Harem

The Ironhaven Pack Series: Wolf Shifter Romances

The Dragon Space Order Bride Series: Sci-Fi Romance

<u>Bears of Crooked Creek</u>: A Bear Shifter Romance Series

<u>Seven Brides For Seven Demons</u>: A Demon Romance Series

<u>Last Warriors of Dilaria</u>: A Sci-Fi Romance Series

The Immortal Blood Series: Vampire Romance

ABOUT CANDICE BUNDY

Candice lives in Denver, Colorado with her son and their cat Newt. A professional hedonist, rabble-rouser, winemaker, and goat-herder, she adores archeology and mythology. Candice focuses on habit hacking to meet minimalist, health, productivity, and positive mojo goals, and sometimes even blogs about it. An unrepentant epicurean, she grows heirloom tomatoes and ferments a variety of sauerkraut, sourdough, kombucha, pickles, and water kefir.

If you would like to know when she has new books out, please sign up for her newsletter here. Email her if the mood strikes you.

For more information:
candicebundy.com
candice@candicebundy.com

ABOUT PIPER FOX

Piper Fox writes steamy paranormal romances for sassy, strong-willed women and the sexy, alpha men who love them.

Follow her on:
Facebook: facebook.com/PiperFoxAuthor
Bookbub: https://www.bookbub.com/profile/piper-fox

www.ingramcontent.com/pod-product-compliance
Lightning Source LLC
Chambersburg PA
CBHW031028190726
48286CB00003BA/1070